PRAISE FOR LITTLE WORLD

"A queer reliquary set adrift on unholy times."
STEPHEN KRAUSE, ALIENATED MAJESTY BOOKS

"*Little World* revolves around a young saint, and women's bodies, lovers, and heartbreak. This is a swift punch of a novella gorgeously written."
CAITLIN LUCE BAKER, ISLAND BOOKS

"A beautiful day trip of a book that sparks marvel over the impenetrable yet quietly persistent mysteries of this world."
MEGHAN COLLINS, LOST CITY BOOKS

"*Little World* is a masterful novel that far exceeds the bounds of its slim size. Josephine Rowe has worked magic here."
STEPHEN SPARKS, POINT REYES BOOKS

"Traveling across time, place, and characters, Rowe tells a story of people encountering divinity and the resulting shifts with tenderness and grace."
BENNARD FAJARDO, POLITICS AND PROSE

"With *Little World*, Rowe has produced her best work yet. A fragmented but vivid narrative, sharpened by jagged lyricism, Rowe's 'little world' feels anything but. This book is an entire universe, unlike anything I've ever read before."
JACOB ROGERS, CENTER FOR FICTION

LITTLE WORLD

Josephine Rowe

TRANSIT
BOOKS

Published by Transit Books
1250 Addison St #103, Berkeley, CA 94702
www.transitbooks.org

© Josephine Rowe, 2025
ISBN: 979-8-893380-16-3 (HC)
Cover design by Jared Bartman | Typesetting by Transit Books
Printed in the United States of America

9 8 7 6 5 4 3 2 1

All rights reserved. This book or any portion thereof may not be reproduced or used in any manner whatsoever without the express written permission of the publisher except for the use of brief quotations in a book review.

LITTLE WORLD

I

Tamanu

The saint is nameless when she comes to Orrin Bird. By horse float, of all things. Though he cannot say what other mode of transport might have been more appropriate, given circumstances. She could hardly have come by rail, accompanied or otherwise. He supposes she might have come by hearse. Though hearses are scarce enough out here, and to receive a casket, a box of any kind from such a vehicle, would have brought attention, prying in the guise of condolences. In fact, condolences are not unwarranted—his old friend, Kaspar Isaksen, is gone, has finally drunk himself to death, and left Orrin custodian to a saint.

Bequest is how she is written up, by Isaksen's solicitor, in the letter that preceded her arrival. The saint had been nameless, even when she'd come to Kaspar. Removed from whatever place she had been kept and cared for, for however long, and where she was presumably entreated by name, one that was lost now. How had she come to Kaspar, on that speck of phosphate in the Central Pacific? Likely no respectable avenue.

Canonization unverified, the letter notes. Then goes on to submit that an incorruptible body, delivered of all evidence of earthly violence and earthly suffering, was still typically considered grounds enough for beatification. Beatification, at the least.

How near or far this places the child from official sainthood, he has no idea. A maybe-saint, a novitiate, a fledgling? The letter is appendixed with a seven-page inventory mounting evidence toward divinity, a litany of saintly characteristics, attributed miracles, the observation of various phenomena—a heady, floral aroma, believed to be the odor of sanctity; attestations to several instances of the eyes appearing to open or close, especially around the solstices. And, on one occasion, the weeping of pink-tinged tears, which were swiftly gathered in a glass lacrimarium, and later blended with chaulmoogra seed oil to create a curative of remarkable potency, alleviating the symptoms of lepers across disparate colonies.

Orrin—not devout, or not in a Catholic sense—is conflicted about the nature of this legacy. He has no notion of how to care for a saint. Even a small one. Does not even believe. Not in any one God, attended by angels and casting His divine judgment down from On High. If he has gods, they are many, and they themselves tend—are the kind who get their hands dirty and wet, who *are* the Dirt and the Wet. And yes, the Dry. Terrible Dry, who doubtless has no comprehension nor will toward terror. Just is. As are the gods Salt and Reef and Ant Mound. The birds who tell him whether he is or isn't home.

Still. Catholic or not. You don't turn away a saint.

He wears his best clothes to receive her, feeling foolish. An olive-green coat that belonged to his father, too heavy for the Kimberley heat. The horse float is fine, as horse floats go. It survives the journey—his house some way from town, and the road neither well made nor well traveled. Two men unhitch the float from their truck and leave it freighted. They speak to one another in a northern language. To Orrin they speak very little. He signs a paper and they leave him with the float.

The interior smells only faintly of the beasts it was intended for. More strongly, to him, it smells of an island church. A scent he's not known for a quarter century, since he left that looted rock for home.

Orrin Bird knows wood. He knows hulls and decks, and the frames of houses. Machines, also, both heavy and light. But mostly he knows wood. The box—coffin-like, after all—is built of canoe timber, tamanu. He recognizes it as his own work. Kaspar had asked for a box, providing exact specifications, twenty-five or more years ago. Said it was for blankets. Tamanu still grew abundant on the island's central plateau then, had not yet been ploughed down in ceaseless gouging for phosphate.

The rigging of his back is still dependable, at sixty-five. When he carries the box into the shade of the house, it seems to weigh less than when first fashioned. Lighter than the planks he'd salvaged and cut for it.

How small is she, inside, and how old? How long did she have in warm, living years? (The letter suggests 11.) And after? In the dormant, closed-in years? The style of her garments supposedly dates to the early eighteenth century, to Europe, but the solicitor's letter allows that they might have been chosen to give the appearance of antiquity. Or, conversely, they might have been serially replaced, updated over time, in accordance with changing fashions or conventions. The garments are painstakingly, tediously described. So she is 11, or she is 250. Or older still, or somewhere between. He does not care to open the box and appraise the garments for himself.

The girl in her box—in the box he built for her, unwitting—warrants a name. Orrin can think only of his mother. His mother was a hard woman. Poured boiling water on the dogs' feed so that they wouldn't wolf it. Her son's, too. But she was a read woman. Countless thick books by Russians, stacked high as the bureau when she was ordered bed rest—he remembers—for the flutter of a sister. The sister did not last. Even so, a name was kept for her. (Was his mother hard, before this? Not known.)

He names the saint for his sister, with no sense of trespass.

He is not versed in the ways of saints. Never having cared for anything but machines and plants and dogs.

Orrin's dogs need only fuel and coaxing words. Dampier dogs, of no discernible breeding. He lets them eat at whatever speeds please them.

First dog, White, returns from wherever she's been, red Pindan dust socking her legs, having stained them that way. Forever, it seems. Again and again, he has sent White dog into the surf, after sticks, to bathe her. Each time, she reemerges looking just the same, but happier.

Second dog, Blue, lags behind in a sore-footed dance, paws stuck full of bindis. Blue dog always finds the bindis. Orrin unsticks them; this is the game.

Let inside the house, the dogs settle immediately in front of the box, and that, to him, is proof enough. He trusts his dogs. He trusts what his dogs trust, bindi patches excepted.

With the saint seen to, overseen, he comes down to the business of missing his friend.

• • •

Of course she has a name, one she was given at birth. And then lived within, almost long enough to get used to it. But that much, the name at least, she is keeping for herself. There are people, still alive, still referring to her by this name. And she is not, has never been, a saint. That hardly needs saying. She is a kid in a box tens of thousands of miles from where she died, with no way back to that place. A kid in a box whose body—*Gott fuck them*—is still somehow of interest to men. When she died, she was already tired of her body being of interest to men. She was fourteen and slight for her age, but that didn't stop them. Did not even slow them down. You'd think death would have taken care of that.

She never learnt to read but could swear in four languages. Five, now. No accounting for it, the way certain things just keep on, banking up. An art to it. An ear. Picking up every shiny dangerous thing dropped from the mouths of canal workers, sailors, in the backstreets of her first city. An ever-expanding arsenal of savage little implements she could conceal on her small person, test the keenness of now and again. Especially on North Americans, milk-soft, with their yellow gases for killing mosquitoes, their pockets full of chewing gum and scraps for cooing strays.

She has always been fond of dogs, and dogs of her. She prefers dogs to people. If she has ever been saint to anyone or anything, it was to one mutt. Who knew what he knew, that dog. Only that when he smelt smoke he went crazy. Running around whimpering with nowhere to go. She protected him from the everyday demon of smoke. He was tiny and hurt and could not return the favor. That was all right. He let her be a kid with a dog. She rubbed the bare pink patches on his haunches and tail, soft as she could.

For the record, it was a very popular name, in her grandmother's time, when her grandmother was a girl. In fact, it was her grandmother's name—there you have it. (Her sister has a daughter, now, and the daughter has her name. It is spoken aloud every day, many times.)

• • •

In her first city, girls her age and younger grew accustomed to the rasp of fresh stubble. Or no, not accustomed to, never really accustomed to: familiar with. Men still shaved, wanted to look respectable to fuck a child. Some girls had tricks to make themselves less girl, less appealing. Wearing their brothers' clothes, for instance. Letting their hair hang in rank snakes, or hacking it away altogether. Walking like maybe they had something you didn't want to catch. Acting wild, plain crazy. She herself was famous at crazy, convincing, bugging her eyes and twitching her limbs and swearing in her several bad languages at imaginary devils whenever a stranger approached. She might have been an actress, might have got around the world that way.

But it happened to her anyhow.

Her sister once told her that every woman who dies like that has already dreamt her death.

And girls?

Girls too. The smart ones.

She was smart. Smarter than most. Had she dreamt her death, then, or one like it? She must have. Stories of that kind went around all the time.

For a time, it had looked like she might yet survive it.

But after it happened. After that happened. Well, after that happens, some said, almost better to die sweet than to live, and grow bitter. They'd seen women grow bitter after living through a thing like that, and no, it was not a pretty sight. It bled your heart. A waste of womanhood, a sinful waste. Better to die sweet, and stay that way.

Death had not sweetened her. It had only enraged her. In death, she grew ever more enraged. The things they'd costumed her in. A joke. A joke and a lie—never in life had she worn anything so elaborately suffocating. Or hideous. Or impractical. If she had been caught going around alive in this froth, someone would have slapped her. Right down from off her high horse. And she hadn't gone into the vault that way, either. Not to begin with. No one had seen the cause for that kind of extravagance. Of course they hadn't.

Incorruptible. Who'd have guessed. (No one, that's who.)

That her body did not corrupt was not miraculous. It was perverse. That her flesh did not retain any trace of violence was a betrayal. It was absolution—she knew about absolution, what and whom it was really for—and if it had been up to her, she would not have given it. If it had been up to her, she would have rained fire and much worse upon that man and all men like him. Called all the ants down from the anthills. Made it slow. If it had been up to her.

It was a curse in some places, some parts of the world: May the earth not eat you.

In older—better—stories, no one is forgiven, and the girl escapes by becoming a tree. A laurel, or a poplar. Or a star. Even a stone—she could settle for being stone.

People once believed that stones could grow, and why not? Limestone was just life heaped up on life heaped up on life and then pressed down hard over millennia. And after all that, people come along and mine it to the surface and grind it to powder and sprinkle it around again in order to call forth more life.

It's a long process. But if you could learn to think in mountaintime, it might come to seem very simple. But people are mostly stupid, very sentimental, very attached to their human time. And even mountains can be annihilated in a matter of puny human years, their insides quarried away for this or for that so in the end they collapse like an old crushed fedora. In the end, it's best not to get too attached, to dogs or mountains, anything at all.

Why not die of yellow fever, like everyone else? Then at least she might have found some peace.

There might still be time to become a tree. If offered a choice, she would prefer tree. Her tree-self would be the kind with poisonous spines that only certain birds and animals could negotiate, and whose fruits appeal only to bats. Needless to mention the armies of fierce stinging ants that would shelter in her limbs and be under her dominion.

• • •

Kaspar Isaksen had been dispatched to the Micronesian island to observe its lazaret: a mile-long stretch of coastline designated for the more infectious cases of Hansen's disease. A byproduct of the phosphate industry, as he saw it, scourge of indentured labor. He had been sent out by a Norwegian university on a three-month appointment, a term he had overstayed by several years. Before this minor mutiny, he had observed at the Dry Stick Colony, Palo Seco, in the Canal Zone. Still held as keepsakes the loose brass and aluminum tokens that were the currency of that place. He had a wife and a son who had accompanied him to Panama—and lived very comfortably as Zonians, it must be said—but who would no longer follow and had since returned to Oslo. The son grown now, in any case. And the wife tending increasingly thorny, and somewhat narrow in her allowances.

The Norwegian was a great admirer of Hansen. He still referred to the malady as Hansen's disease, though most physicians called it leprosy. He still referred to the island as Pleasant, though its people called it Naoero. Its remoteness made conditions for study exceptionally favorable.

Could a lazaret be made cheerful? Might the isolated come to feel less isolated, even content, within its confines? Kaspar—who had been accorded no official title or duty by the Administration, but who nevertheless believed the residents of the colony lay under his Protection—aided in the scheduling of brass bands and picture shows and games of itsibweb, whose ball was contrived from a rock wound around and around with pandanus leaves. There was rarely a bloodless match. He distributed reading material that trickled in secondhand from well-wishers in Australia and New Zealand. Conversations with unafflicted friends and relations were permitted at a distance of sixteen feet. He learnt much from the lee side.

Orrin had first come to the island to work on equipment that made other, distant men rich, other land rich, and the land he stood on poor, snaggled, Martian. Then he worked for Kaspar, doing far less, and less harm. Simple carpentry with simple tools, or sorting donations for the colony.

Kaspar brewed a tea that had the likeness of pale-green oil, very bitter, whose effect was soporific. Some cautioned against the invitation to drink, warned that the stuff would suppress a man's spirit and leave him susceptible to the biddings of the Norwegian. Orrin half believed them. And he drank anyway. He is unsure whether his will was corrupted during that time. They never shared a bed through a full night. Waking alone, he rarely felt shame.

Kaspar had accumulated the names of all the birds on the island, in Nauruan and in English, and would offer these upon sight or sound. Thus, Orrin Bird received the names of all the birds. But their calls kept him awake in the darkness, unnerved him. He'd lie there, alert and seething. Once or twice he opened a window and threw something. If he'd had a gun. Yes, he would have. Shot the bloody things down to earth. (He'd knocked once, in the riotous dawn dark, on Kaspar's door, and asked to borrow his rifle. Kaspar knew better than to let him, sent him away placated with some new concoction for sleep.)

The Norwegian assented to eating fish from the sea but saw no reason in causing profitless harm to any creature. During crab time, when the lowlands were a sideways-shifting carpet of crustaceans, the older man erected temporary plank walkways so as not to crush them underfoot. He adopted the local sport of luring and taming frigates. Their purring clicks and croaks were a soothing timpani to Kaspar, to most others. Not to Orrin.

In the Kimberley, it's never been that way. Here, where the birds call up dawn with just as much clamor, they've always sounded sweet to him. Even the shrillest. Even when they roust him from sleep. They'll just as likely soothe him back.

Maybe that's how you know where home is. The birds don't chivy you so much.

Night; the saint in the kitchen. The dogs, for once, do not scratch at his door to get into his bed. Of course he dreams her. And when she appears, it is not in the burden of deep velvet and Alençon lace, nor the rich silks as inventoried in the letter. Nor the ridi, nor any other exotic flourish.

The saint, the girl, Irina, is dressed in ordinary linen, sweat- and salt-stiff, dark circles under her eyes, already. Born tired. She is brusque and without patience for fools or penitents. Pushes her long, dark hair from her face with a fury that is familiar to him. She pours forth from a ragbag of languages, of which he understands only a little, a few intermittent words, mostly the swearing. She curses precociously. She curses blue murder. Profanities suited to sailors and miners, blasphemy inflected by the German *Gott*, the French *putain*. She goes barefoot at the height of the day, over the scorching claypans and with the baking red dirt swilling up to her ankles. Goes slowly and unflinching, as no stranger to this place, to this dust, ever could.

Apart from this inviolability, he suspects that she is not miraculous, that she is of no greater faith or sanctity than he. He does not say so.

On waking, he has no desire either to confirm this vision or to relinquish it. No desire to open the tamanu box and compare the dream image to the earthly, incorruptible stuff. He desires, in fact, not to. Fears she will not return.

Among his other, more practical fears: that white ants will devour the box. Their pillars rise up sentinel from the surrounding scrub, advancing in stature and girth by the year. He keeps the habit of measuring, with tape and logbook. Refers to them by character, or cardinal, or by simple reference point. *Mammoth: nearest to water tank. Goliath: seaward. David: east of Goliath.* He places his ear to their pocked hulls, fancies he can hear their industry.

Certain times—at the brief, colorless edges of the day—their ghostly forms put him in mind of the crags and pinnacles of fossilized coral, the chewed-out core of the eviscerated island, gouged up and hauled away to be processed for fertilizer. Though whatever the hour, and whether lit by sun or moon, those exhausted Nauruan monoliths resembled tombstones. Unlike the ant homes, they had no resonance, no language, told of no cloistered animation within. Only of depletion—a boneyard that expanded steadily, by the year.

The work that had taken him there was instrumental to this decimation. The island, encircled by reef, had no harbor. The cantilever was three years' construction. At last, its gargantuan insectile arms swung over the barricade of coral and then back out to the freighters anchored offshore, bearing crushed phosphate at a thousand tons an hour.

Yes, it was impressive to witness, a feat of engineering. And yes, the dust powdered everything. Orrin wheezed in it. He'd come to this trade because his shallow lungs were no good for diving. Nor were they good for any war.

His father had pearled, and fought, and sailed back from the Western Front to pearl again. Eventually, the sea just kept hold of him. Something Orrin remembers of his father: he would not speak of the front, but during thunderstorms was given to recall the great cannonade of Krakatoa—which could be heard even from Perth—and the incomparable sunsets that came after. The persistent ring around the sun, and how folk then spoke of the End. But it wasn't the End. So, there you have it, his father said: sometimes it looks like the End, but it isn't.

It was the End somewhere, put in Orrin's mother, from behind her book. For a great lot of folk, that was the End. Then she dipped her head back into Tolstoy's Russia.

Kaspar once told Orrin that he had the air of a man brought up among sisters. This was not intended as insult; Orrin did not take it as insult. Though he had no sisters, only the enduring apparition of one.

• • •

It's true that her eyes might open on occasion. Or appear to open, to whoever might be looking. This is a common enough phenomenon, in accordance with measurable exterior factors such as ambient temperature and humidity. When they brought her to the Kimberley, into the Dry, her eyelids shrank. Simple. In the Kimberley, her eyes are open more than half the year.

But in short, it makes no difference.

To speak of consciousness: complicated. What does she know, from this near remove? More and less. Her awareness is disengaged from human senses, is beyond human senses, but only so far. Not as far as could be hoped. Her little world.

Evening, when the house is thrown open to the westerly, and some skerrick of it steals in through the slats of tamanu, rustles the layers enveloping her within the box, it can't exactly be said that she feels the breeze cool on her skin. Only a recognition that there is breeze, that it comes from the west, that such a breeze would feel cool upon the skin. An awareness that the man, Orrin Bird, feels the breeze as cooling to his skin; that the dogs pant their relief into it, exchanging it for their hot yawns. It can be said that this is enjoyable, that satisfaction of a kind is still available to her. The man, Orrin, inclining his gray-ginger head, spreading his hands as if in praise, reaching into the current of air as if into a stream of water. She cannot know what her sister is doing. Sometimes, she hears her name.

Hears? To put it differently:

Sometimes, there is her name.

Her sister told of at least one woman who'd tried to fake her way into the leper colony, back in the Canal Zone. Life didn't cost anything there. And it was good enough for Americans.

At the Palo Seco colony, her sister prepared meals and medicines, crushing ripe chaulmoogra seeds into oil. She swam in the lepers' sea, where others would never dare, for fear that the bacteria would wash down and infect them, the Clean.

The Norwegian watched her swim, and asked why she was not afraid. She had never been afraid, but even in her grief—proud idiot—she had to brag. She swiped the water from her limbs with the firm blade of her hand and answered: My sister is incorruptible.

And that did it. The Norwegian was all packed up for Micronesia. But he asked to visit the girl saint.

He was shown to where they had her laid out in that monstrous costume.

I see, he said. My word.

There was still the tedious matter of veneration, obtaining official recognition from the Church. The requisite petitioning, locally and abroad, miracles to be recorded and attested to, relics to be examined. Bureaucracies that ran far beyond the family's means and station.

Yes, of course he could assist. Use his standing and considerable etcetera etcetera, advance proceedings.

He was packed and ready, but he quietly made arrangements for more effects.

There are relics, you could call them that. They are objects of absolutely no use or importance to her: a comb, a holy book, some tacky beads and ornaments. (Why not weapons, something practical? Why not a knife, or a spear, or a sword edged with sharks' teeth?)

Other earthly things, still with her, more valuable:

The crackle and slow spill of honeycomb, snatched cool from storage, bitten into on a hot morning.

The tug of her sister's fingers combing her hair with a bright-smelling balm, impatient but not ungentle.

Her own fingers sifting the shore, slivers of coral and ossified wood slipping through.

The ocean carrying her on its breath.

• • •

When Orrin returned to Western Australia from Micronesia, the Tasmanian tiger was newly extinct, and his mother had lost the words for simple things. Handed a teacup, she'd call it a chaucer. You had to laugh, except when you couldn't. In his mind, these losses were linked, threads of a greater diminishing.

And then another war. He was too old by then for his bad lungs to matter. Japan bombed Darwin in the summer of '42, and strafed Broome two weeks later. Roebuck Bay skeined with burning oil, and flying boats blazing down into it, laden with Dutch refugees bound for sanctuary.

Letters arrived; Kaspar had removed himself to New Zealand, to Manawatu and whatever distant family he had there, to wait out the worst of it. Nauru had been subject to several raids, by air and by sea. Kaspar did not see its occupation. At last, he missed his homeland. His wife and his son. Still, it was the island he vowed a return to, whatever might be left of it, once the war closed down.

Orrin's mother died believing the war would last forever. Did that matter? No, it was all the same war anyway. Sometimes it looked like the End, but it wasn't.

(Hiroshima. Nagasaki. For a great lot of folk: yes.)

In the years that followed, Kaspar Isaksen took up the task of methodically drinking himself to death. His letters came clogged with remorse for fates he'd not learnt of until after the war. For instance how, during the occupation, his former charges had been rounded up on their cultivated strip of coast and loaded into small boats, and the boats towed out to sea, shelled, and sunk. Thus leprosy was removed from the island. He had withdrawn his Protection, he scratched, in a script crouched by shame and by guilt, and his wards had suffered the greatest consequence.

Protection. Orrin initially reckoned the capitalization a Scandinavian slip by the inebriated Norwegian, nothing to do with divinity. Kaspar's correspondence made no other allusion to the saint, even then.

What could a lone man have done? would have been Orrin's reply. *Been drowned alongside, like the rest?*

But he had not replied.

Now, understanding what was meant by Protection, he might simply have gestured toward Europe: teeming with saints, and still full of bomb craters.

• • •

The first box was formed of rough planks, birch. It carried her across the North Pacific, away from her isthmus.

She knew the lives of those birches, before they were planks.

For a tree, being a box is much the same as being a saint: your own life is over, but people are still bothering you, expecting you to help. She felt bad for the birch.

This box is built of boat wood. But placed half a day's walk from water. In any case, it isn't properly sealed; air gets in. What is she supposed to do, out here?

Sometimes, he leaves the radio on.

Sometimes, there is her name.

• • •

If she had survived, she might still be alive. Middle-aged, now. Grown bitter, but perhaps loved for it, even so. Bitter has its merits, its sophistications. Bitter is a rite, a taste you can acquire. People go to some trouble to acquire a taste for it. It's something. Sweet is nothing. Sweet is for children, for a child squatting on a stone floor with a stolen honeycomb. A minor art made of melting and dividing nectar from wax in her mouth, spitting out the hard globs to save for wax animals.

But then, she might not have been bitter at all. She might have been formidable, and worldly. She might have brought down fire and ants and worse, and then simply stepped away and left them to it. Made the same passage by choice, upright, in simple linen. Not as cargo. Might have come all this way out of wanderlust, just because she felt like it, then planted her hands and feet in the red soil and grown here.

She might have passed by this man, his blue dog and his dirty white dog, and they would have regarded one another, briefly and without obligation, and wished well, and gone on.

• • •

Every few summers, cyclones come to thrash the region, and his house is spared. He does not believe the girl is a saint. He does not believe she is his sister. And yet, and yet.

For the seventeen years left to him, he dreams most nights of her small, furious face, and wakes now and then with the feeling of polished stones slipping cool through his fingers, a sound like rain or the wind that shows the pale undersides of leaves, set at the edge of knowing something of magnitude. For seventeen years, he wakes with the feeling and lets the feeling dim, lets it go. Then he gets up, feeds the dogs, goes out into the dark to piss, tows the dinghy to the sea, puts the dinghy on the water, and waits. Says his sister's name aloud, sometimes, in greeting or parting, never entreats her for anything more.

He lives small amid the ant mounds, constructs a greenhouse of salvaged windows and sheet plastic to cultivate seeds carried home in his pockets, many years before, varieties he suspects no longer grow on the island from which he gathered them. No noteworthy harm comes to him before his time, by which point it is not met as harm. The dogs, White and Blue, are long since. He passes on without will or testament. He makes no provision or instruction for the girl, the maybe-saint.

In his absence, the radio continues to broadcast its cycle of near and distant despair, until the battery runs down.

Then for a long time, no human voices, only those remembered.

Around the house, the ant mounds grow in stature and girth. White ants do not eat the box. White ants do not care for tamanu. They devour instead: the stumps and joists, the posts and beams. The floor goes soft. The veranda gives way. The roof buckles in on itself. The ant mounds grow in stature, and in girth.

The greenhouse lasts longer than it should, until the plastic is brittled by the Dry, ribboned by the Wet. The plants wither and crisp. Rabbits and possums chew what's left down to the roots.

Now and then, an animal thumping through the ruin of what had once been a house, a bird preparing its home above a lintel. She is aware of the sea drawing closer.

II

Eigenlicht

Matti, the others have taken to calling her, somewhere during the drive across the center. Her full name too feminine maybe, or too stale. Or just too German, even for '76. The other two, Suze and Alex, are both in their twenties. This trip is a lark. She's thirty-six, wonders if she's too old for this, too old for larks. But she has never seen the desert.

Matti. She tries it on.

Suze and Alex aren't far out of university, with lives that will wait for them, qualifications that will keep, their possessions stowed with parents in comfortable suburbs.

But what she envies them most is their ability to sleep. Anywhere, it seems: sitting upright in the van, or near-comatose in a storm-thrashed tent. On a blanket in the sun, curled up like puppies, together more often than not. Half undressed, their nipples and bellies exposed to the sky in public parks, church grounds, memorial lawns. Immune to male attention of any kind, oblivious to both wolf whistles and slurs. *Show some fucken respect, you little whores.* It's only Matti who hears, heats up, draws her arms closer to her fully clothed body.

She is accustomed to being the only one awake. Has not slept through a full night in a long time. Possibly decades. Wonders how her life might be if she could achieve this one simple act, this common mercy. Seven, even six solid hours a night—how she might spend that clarity. She imagines assurance drawn from the fixed forms of things, their clean, unambiguous delineations.

Maybe that was the dream, though, the great illusion: that of separateness.

Until this drive, she had never seen the desert. Now she feels an affinity, especially with the early light, its brittle greengold, the edges of supposedly solid things dissolving into the vast expanses between. The hours when all seems of the one substance, before the sun arrives to blast everything into ruthless and lonely distinction.

Seventeen days on the road. At some point, she has become the helmsman. This might have been the intention from the start, when the younger two invited her to join, to divvy up the fuel and the driving. Or it might be the natural order of things. Even though they'd met on equal footing—Monday night meetings on nonviolent resistance at the Mechanics'. (Charcoal dust on the floor of the old Hall, used fits in the bathroom, laminated AA credo tacked up above the steel sink.)

In any case, she is accustomed. She pilots many miles—or, they're calling them kilometers now—whole landscapes while the other two sleep. Sometimes feels she is the night watchman, sole witness to the complicated logic of their dreams, their mumbled sleeptalk, body gripes, unmuffled sex sounds, orgasms not quite stifled by the foam mattress laid in back.

Matti stays awake with the sharp smell of refresher towelettes hoarded from truck stops, petrol and metal and steering wheel smells lingering on her hands. Fingering the coin slots of pay phones when no one is looking. Habit. She was raised with Hunger and it will never, never leave her. Even so. Even so, she still feels chosen by moments of Grace—being filled or enfolded or directed by it. She wonders to whom or what the Grace belongs. Hunger, she sometimes believes. A vastness. The emptiness of glaciers or of the desolate transit halls of evacuated cities. Pictures her parents have put in her head.

Driving the long straight, the newly sealed highway stretched taut as catgut, her thoughts are like crossed wires. Distant, unfamiliar voices drifting in through a receiver and charged with the same freakish urgency. With sleeplessness comes the shimmer of clairvoyance that attaches itself to everything, to the otherwise ordinary and incidental. Birds lifting from the body of a flattened snake as if from a slack wire, chips of yellow reflector plastic on the bitumen, abandoned bassinet in the roadside weeds, empty Fanta can crushed under the accelerator pedal. In the heat haze and the grainy dawns and phosphorescent twilights, the *eigenlicht*—her father's word for the fizzing and dissolving gray particles. A sense of déjà vu; something going on in the brain, going wrong. Some synapse or other inhibited, misfiring. There's a neurological explanation for it, she's sure. She'll look into that when she's back in Melbourne, in reach of the library.

Or maybe she won't. Maybe she'll leave it as a mystery, something just for herself, her sleepless self. The glimmer of pre-destiny, the detached faith it allows.

Faith?

Acceptance.

She looks much older than she is. It's okay. It is. One day she will simply conk out. She accepts this, too.

Thirty-six. At times it occurs to her that all of this—the highway, the van, the West Australian glare, the arrhythmic ticking of the dodgy indicator—is bowing toward the close of the second act in a three-act play. If her life were a three-acter, the first would have ended with giving away the boy. Or, no, it would end with the few precious and bitter hours spent alone with him outside the Home. Taking him by train into the city, just to have him circumcised, then delivering him right back into the custody of the Little Sisters. There were some minutes, a quarter hour stolen, sitting with a hot chocolate in a city laneway café, just her feet and one arm in the sun. Her baby boy in the shade. Looking into his face, trying to read it for betrayal, distrust. Finding nothing.

Or that opening act could just as well end a few days later, after he had been given over—to *a wonderful life*, to *every opportunity*—and she was left with her stitches and slack belly crying in Sally's arms. But Sally was already gone by then, too. She had cried and wished for Sally's arms. No rewriting the past. Beyond the inescapable revisions and elisions of memory. She had been given a few days' rest (*Grace*) to collect herself, and then been sent back into the world, delivered of moral danger and violently heartsick. Her confused body too empty and too full at once, heavy with needless milk, a chasmal hollowing at her center. The name she gave him would only be temporary, she knew, for the certificate. They said better not to give him one that mattered too much. That seemed stingy, though. As if she were sending him out into bad weather half-dressed, just to keep a good coat dry. She named him Eliot.

That was that. End Act One.

She knows the tropes of three-act plays. Brecht, Ibsen. Chekhov—the protagonist announcing themselves and showing their open palms to the audience, the gun on the wall from the first act going off in the third.

Anything could be the gun on the wall. Sally could be the gun on the wall.

There was always the hope. Some small secret readiness, protected.

· · ·

Seventeen days, in motion or baking in car parks, campsites. The van is a decade old, in faded gray-green. Seafoam, Suze calls it. Mildew, says Alex, whose brother has loaned it while drifting around Asia, nurturing a dope habit he'd picked up as a Nasho in Vietnam.

Suze is their radio, when the radio is on the blink, or the signal drops away. Sweat-stiff batik and her slim dirty feet up on the dash, she wavers through "Song to the Siren," "The Calvary Cross." Alex in the back, threatening to throttle her if she doesn't switch to something more upbeat. She wants Patti Smith's "Gloria," Bowie's "Starman," wants something a bit less blow-your-sad-soggy-brains-out, if you don't mind. Alex mostly supine in her backseat fiefdom, issuing decrees to the front while stretched out on the grubby mattress as if loafing on a palanquin. Carsick, or pretending to be. Though on solid ground, at camp, she is always on her feet, the self-appointed pitcher of tents, hauler of water, builder and stoker of campfires. Even prostrate she busies herself rolling cigarettes, rolling joints, passing them forward. Cocooned in the soft Nicaraguan hammock she strings up at each campsite to lie naked in, sipping on a tea brewed from shriveled mushrooms, which she claims enables her to live on sunlight alone for days at a time. Matti can almost believe it. Has tried the tea, just a mouthful, which tasted exactly like dirt. Has seen Alex standing stripped down in the light between trees, as raddly as a branch herself. Eyes closed, face upturned toward the sun like a heliotrope, hands floating slowly upward from her sides, as if with the swell of unheard music or rising water.

• • •

The smell inside the van is of unwashed clothes and cola spills, coffee spills, hash oil and cigarettes, desiccating foam, campfire smoke and sebum and Suze's bottle of Chanel something-or-other that she periodically spritzes everything with, which to Matti just smells like dirty sugar.

Matti listens to the backseat polemics on class mobility and workers' rights and women's rights, all the limelight that Greer takes up and who else might be filling it and with what. Uranium mines, covert nuclear test sites, Tasmanian wilderness battles and the Jungian psychoanalyst whose sleek East Melbourne couch they both visit weekly (a friend of Alex's father, who is also an analyst). They are both interested in dreams, their murky underworkings, and in ripping them to bits. Matti lies and says that even when she does sleep, she can't remember her dreams, although this too is grounds for dissection. Verdict: probably repression.

If you don't dream you go batshit, says Alex, matter-of-fact. There are studies. If you don't sleep at all you just croak from exhaustion, simple, but if you sleep and don't dream you don't process anything, and it's too much. You just lose your shit, she finishes, opening a hand in a starburst beside her temple.

Right, Matti says. Well, you two let me know.

Lately her dreaming—or at least her highway-mind, her uprooted and roving consciousness—has returned to the Home. The dreams she had there, recurring, of waking at night and wading into the stubborn current of the river, disappearing quietly beneath its swirling eddies of brown froth. This was never disquieting. Not a dream of drowning as such, but of epiphany, almost of homecoming. The recovery of something important and collectively forgotten. Always she'd wake with the phantom of lost knowledge clinging to her, akin with the sensation of the thin bedsheets and cotton nightie plastered to her hot skin, drenched in dreaming with river water and in waking with summer sweat.

Or she'd wake to Sally, to Sally's heat soaking into her, Sally's smell, grassy and sharp. Sally's wet voice close to her ear.

I only came cause you called out.

True? Though she didn't really care if it was true. Sally's legs endless, it seemed, wrapped around hers in the dark. Protective or possessive, she didn't mind about that either. Her belly round and firm, insistent between them, her tits still very small, like a runner's or a dancer's. Sally would wet three fingers in her mouth and slip them down inside, talking the whole way through, words swallowed up in the dark, as Mathilde's body responded and her neck tipped forward of its own volition. She thought of kittens turning limp when you lifted them between thumb and forefinger, or—*click*—the puppet-like slump of the hypnotized.

Doesn't mean you're bent or anything, Sally said. Or not for always. Just gotta make our own fun while we're in here.

• • •

The second act might open with hands. Her own, plunging ungloved into buckets of White King, Mondays through Fridays, scouring the everyday grit of living from the houses of the wealthy. Eroding the ridges and whorls of her own fingerprints. Her parents no longer spoke to her, ashamed, but for some years she still spoke with traces of their accent and her employers wanted to know what side they'd been on, whether her folks had tattoos, where she was born.

We came before all that, was all she offered. I was born here.

And if pressed further, she might clarify: Swiss German. Or, German-speaking Swiss, which seemed to be heard more favorably. A half-truth, either way. They were German-speaking Germans, who had fled briefly to Luzern just before the war, which they rarely spoke of.

The war filtered into the household in other ways—in the abhorrence of excess, a vehement distrust of appetite. And in somber preparedness for Real hunger, for a time when it might once again arrive to ringbark their lives. Mathilde had never known Real hunger, her parents made clear. May never in her life know Real hunger, God willing, thanks either to their prayers or to their vigilance—the house was stockpiled with food, provisioned like an air-raid shelter, cupboards stacked with tins of peaches and apricots, condensed and evaporated milk, rice pudding, home preserves, tomatoes, sardines, pasta—but to eat to satisfaction was equivalent to gluttony, and to admit to hunger after being fed was an ingratitude, as well as a confirmation of psychological and spiritual deficiency.

The lower order of hunger that Mathilde nevertheless felt and attempted to conceal was, all the same, consuming. A cold, hollow ache that had its own force, one that moved her beyond fear or reason. She tried to temper it with prayer, or, when prayer did not work, to redirect it to lesser offences—chewing mouthfuls of desiccated coconut or spent coffee grounds, or furtively stripping blossoms from the honeysuckle vine that tumbled over the back fence—until inevitably the desire became greater than her stunted self, larger than shame or consequence: the darkness that was her mother, storming down the hallway, blotting out the transom light to slap whatever it was out of her hands, then to slap her face, sticky with peach syrup or condensed milk. But not before a pure and private relish had swept through her—flavors and textures enhanced by longing, that flooded and overwhelmed her heightened senses, her sharpened, illegitimate appetite.

A relish that could not be threatened or beaten out of her, as it turned out.

Though long out of her parents' home, part of her still braced for impact, the full-body memory of her mother charging up. She ate slowly in the presence of others, a watchful anticipation that caused her shoulders to stiffen and her jaw to clench, involuntarily, so that she sometimes had difficulty swallowing, and barely tasted, so focused was she on the complicated mechanics.

Only when eating alone, unguarded, could she recover that deeper sense of relish she felt as a child, before the darkness rushed in.

Are you a breatharian or something? Alex asked, fireside one night, staring as Matti speared up individual chickpeas and die-sized bites of vegetable from the shadows of her graniteware bowl.

You eat like a mouse, she went on, then made an awful rattish snicking sound.

I'm just not used to this much spice, Matti said, and laid aside her bowl and cutlery. Eating impossible now, under scrutiny. Her stomach clenching in refusal, *No*.

Her hunger was its own clarifying force, a secret but not, not anymore, a shameful one. She had decided, long ago, to form an allegiance with it.

Maybe too simple, too tidy for this now to be approaching the third and final act, her life snapped neatly into eighteen-year increments. Or maybe fitting: institutional. Fifty-four would seem young for it all to stop. Young, maybe, but not so tragic, not so near. Eighteen more years an eternity to Mathilde. Time enough for everything to be recovered. Or rather buried and broken down, left to decay and regenerate. If she were to have another child, now, or even soon, they'd know her well enough by fifty-four. They would know that Hunger was its own form of faith.

• • •

When they reach the west coast, there will be whale sharks. Possibly swimming with whale sharks. The three of them agree on this much, even if the itinerary from that point is indeterminate, beyond a vague sense of north. That is the hope: Ningaloo Reef, whale sharks, and from there, perhaps the Kimberley, followed by some hazy image of Alice.

For now, Matti pilots, Suze and Alex high as cats' backs and synchronizing in a low atonal humming. Communing, or maybe invoking something. It sounds somewhere between test pattern and whale song. Whale sharks, Matti thinks, though she has no idea what kind of song they might make, or even if they have song.

A retired carnival man in a Kingston caravan park had blessed Suze's SX-70 to always capture the true essence of whoever was framed in the viewfinder.

Matti covets the camera, despite knowing she could not afford the film. It would be like having a flashy car you couldn't refuel, an exotic animal you couldn't feed.

Along the way Suze shoots Polaroid portraits of Matti and Alex, their smeared likenesses as if seen through rained-on glass. Haloed in wild coronas of colored light, like icons.

Your auras, Suze says, convinced of her work.

It's only a trick, Matti knows—Suze pushing the emulsions around with her hot fingers before the images are fixed. The colors blooming up from somewhere underneath like fate before she lifts her hands away, assessing the result, the broody gloaming tones and the visceral, crepuscular purples.

Shots of Alex taken from above, slung out in her hammock recumbent and blissed, flaring orange and red-gold. Stoned smile flashing her cat's tooth, making a double *V* sign with her fingers.

Alex always turns out the brighter, the more glorious of the two.

The photographs of Matti are all taken with her at the wheel, attention fixed rigidly on the highway ahead, jaw tight with discomfort or features blurred from turning her face away, reflexively. Every one of these enveloped by an inky bloom of dark opal blues, as if the endless wakeful nights had seeped in for keeps.

Alex leans in from the back, rests her sharp chin on Suze's shoulder. What's indigo mean?

Depends, really. It can mean wisdom. Independence, loyalty, sensitivity. Heightened intuition. But the darker bits, the greeny black here? Suze traces with her pinkie fingernail. That can also mean past violence, spiritual oppression.

It's a decision, Matti knows. To see her this way. She watches Suze's fingers describe the edges of her face, caressing, interfering with the chemistry. If she were to press her fingertips there just a little harder, or a little longer—Matti isn't sure of the method—the colors might say something completely different.

Or maybe indigo just means thirst, Suze offers in late, limp kindness.

Bullshittttterrrrr, Alex purrs, and slides her tongue into Suze's ear. Suze crinks her neck in mock disgust, before turning her mouth to meet Alex's.

Anyway, Alex says, flopping back onto the mattress with a deep sigh. We're all fucking thirsty.

They hadn't been sleeping together—Matti is almost certain—when they'd set out from Melbourne. It had started around Port Augusta, probably. The motel there: bleach-stained towels, cardboard walls hung with faded prints of native wildlife warped behind plexiglass frames. Spectral wombats and echidnas ambling forth from cyan underbrush. Matti's room had been across the car park from theirs. She hadn't heard anything. But when they set out again in the morning something had shifted, the geometry skewed, and she understood herself to be set at the periphery, a satellite. A not unfamiliar, almost comfortable position; from the margins one might more easily slip away, unnoticed and undetained.

Their preoccupation with one another is, she has decided, a kind of blessing. Allows space for what the Little Sisters would have called Kenosis, what the Buddhists call Śūnyatā, and what the Taoists call The Ten Thousand Things, which certain metaphysicians call Contemplation of the Void, and more importantly honors her mother's living and dying wish: that she not draw attention to herself.

She expects, has expected all along, that at some point they will find an excuse to continue on to Alice without her. That she will make the journey back to Melbourne alone, sitting upright the whole way; a three-day rail trip on the line that cuts through the bright-red guts of the country. She knew this going in—or it felt like knowing—and so had brought with her only what she could comfortably shoulder, or abandon.

The rail line runs through Kalgoorlie, and it would be desert, the real desert then. Edge of the parched bed of what was once sea, now studded with opalized remnants of Cretaceous sea creatures stranded far inland—fossils corresponding to indigenous lore of great tidal waves and floods, knowledge that was already ancient at the time of the Noah stories.

• • •

When Mathilde first arrived at the Home—The Blue House, they called it—a Sister showed her the grounds. The Blue House was touted as both refuge and adoption agency, although in most lights the old homestead looked the gunmetal gray of a prison hulk, and stood just as removed. The property was in sight of the city but a world apart, out of reach and out of temptation, enclosed within acres of market gardens, orchards that stretched until the eye was thwarted by water or by ranks of poplars and pines that stood as windbreaks. Nowhere to run even if you were thinking of it, and anyway better than elsewhere.

Cordoned off from the rest of civil, God-fearing society by nectarines and plums, pious rows of lettuces and beans.

Here's how we earn our keep, Sister was saying.

The revenue from adoptions went unmentioned. Mathilde imagined them swaddled there among the cabbages, or being pulled up like beetroots, red faced and ready to bawl.

She could smell the wet of the leaves, both green and fallen, crushed into mud, the wet of the closed sky and unseen stock animals, the river glimpsed through trees, moving slow and brown beyond the greenhouses and stables and milking sheds.

Sally had been out in the garden. Tall. She glanced but did not greet, busy putting hessian sacks over young fruit trees. It looked like preparations for a medieval execution. But it was for their own good, Sister explained. There'd been a false spring, and things had started blooming prematurely.

Like us, hey, Sister? The older girl spoke now, tonguing a sharp incisor, and the nun shook her head and turned away.

They were each of them Girls in Moral Danger. Though it was already clear that the danger was thought greater in Sally, and likely intractable.

Can't tear the Devil out of her kind—Sister Adeline was wheezing—can only scare it off the threshold for a minute. Her face averted, her form a shapeless black flapping that Mathilde followed up the marshy ground toward the house.

Mathilde turned back and watched as the older girl, slowly and with an unnerving reverence, raised the damp brown sack she'd been holding to cover the swell of her belly.

She was further along than Mathilde, who brought her hand to her own stomach, instinctively.

Sally looked at her, held her eyes.

And who the fuck are you? she said, or the look said. Sally whipped the sack away from her middle like a bored toreador, and went back to swaddling the fruit trees.

• • •

My name is Mathilde Eberhart, she says now to the desert dark, to the flattened snake, to the gun-barrel highway and the treeless plain. And these are my hands. She lifts her hands from the steering wheel, lays her palms flat against the windscreen, and watches the speedometer rising like an answer. Like Hunger, like Grace.

• • •

There were ten or a dozen there at any time, a revolving cast of unwed and underage women in various stages of gestation and disgrace, who lacked the means or connections or the nerve for backyard abortionists.

Though some had diligently tried, themselves, with dried straws of seaweed, self-inseminations of soapy water, galloping hell for leather on borrowed horses over broken-up country. There were the weirder wives' tales:

mountains of apricots heaped under a bed, bitter elixirs of yarrow and clove, liberal doses of white pepper and castor oil. Prayers and offerings to Saint Hildegard of Bingen, whose tongue and heart lay housed in gold on the other side of the world, but who might mercifully bestow a miscarriage, even at that remove, if she happened to pick up the message (who knew where her ears were).

The more tenacious and pragmatic among them had simply utilized knitting needles and crochet hooks, though clearly not to sufficient effect.

Rare among them, those who had not tried at all, even with prayer—a small number of them God- and hell-fearing. Though threats of damnation less persuasive than the grim horror stories of septicemia or bleeding out on bathroom floors after being seen to by back-alley quacks.

Mathilde had considered such options, those few that were available to her. But she hadn't tried, or even willed to lose him, in the end. She'd thought there might be a little time left to make up her mind. Say, for instance, it had happened differently . . . then what? Although even in her alternate versions, the tapering corral of her imagination somehow delivered her here: to this place or a place like it, or a worse place.

Sally had no need of implements, or Saint Hildegard. She had no intention of growing her baby to full, only to deliver him into the arms of some rich white saviors. She said she had the knowledge to take care of that. The baby would just have to come back another year. Its spirit would understand, hang back a bit. Nature could do like that. If conditions turned ugly, everything in nature might just hang back a bit. Simple.

You don't believe me, hey, Sally said.

Only, she did. She knew Sally was not talking about laminaria or knitting needles. This was something else.

You afraid of me sometimes, Little Sister?

Little Sister, a neat stab at herself and the nuns, in one. Sally wasn't even a full year older. But yes, Mathilde was afraid. Not of Sally exactly but of what she rucked up in her. Some force, some kind of current, mercurial. Kissing Sally was like pressing her tongue to a nine-volt battery.

Or else, Sally called her Vanilla. Or Baby Vanilla. Vanilla meant several things at once, apparently: that she was pale, that she was plain, that she was sweet. Probably that she was naive, or worse—innocent. That she didn't know anything. As if they weren't in the exact same place for the exact same reason.

She was, she understood then—might always be—the kind of person that people felt entitled to nickname, right off the bat. What that says about her, she doesn't know. She has never felt the right to give anyone else a nickname. Even Sally was just Sally.

What they'd have done, the Sisters.

Matti wonders, even now, what would have happened if they were found out.

Send one or both of them away, obviously. Likely to shock therapy.

Aberrant, abhorrent, deviant.

But they weren't found out, weren't dogged on. Small mercy of her life, that they weren't, that this transgression went unpunished.

Except that it was, in a way; she never saw Sally after.

And she'd been right, Sally. Her baby didn't last.

That's just stuff, Sally assured, her long legs slick down the insides, but she looked afraid behind her hard mouth. Mathilde knew how to see it.

The feel of her belly afterward, still there, but sagging softer.

And then Sally herself was gone, out. Free.

Her own baby, the boy, would be a man now. Almost. Old enough for war, when the next one rolled in, and they brought the lotteries back. Her heart a cold stone in her stomach during the televised birthday ballots for Vietnam, like bad science fiction, or a kind of modern paganism.

Would she know him? In Melbourne, riding the trams out to work in Kew, in Camberwell, peering into the faces of university students on the 16 tram, on the 72. But it was up to him, to do the looking—if he knew, and cared to look. She had given him a name at birth, but the name would have been changed.

These are the things she knows better than to share. There are some things, many things in fact, that she has gotten away with this long by keeping them close, unspoken. And more besides that she has managed to keep at distance even from herself, simply by refusing them the language that would enable them to put down roots, make a home of her.

At least she'd known it, what it felt like. Of being that full, of being more than her small self. She decides that this, too, is a kind of Grace. Then she wills it gone, grays it out, lets it dissolve into particles above the Eyre.

The other two have come up in leafy inner suburbs, old houses with names above the numbers, which Matti also knows the insides of, via the grit. Knows, more or less, how Alex and Suze's childhood bedrooms would have looked, where their treasures and their shames were hidden. They would still have been children when she went to work cleaning such places. Comfortable homes—a word that wealthy people use when they hope not to embarrass those considerably less comfortable than themselves.

Sometimes she believes she has already met them, or their younger selves, in Kew, in Malvern. At least glimpsed them, adolescent and languid, through bay windows of diamond-beveled glass, lounging by backyard pools during listless summer holidays. Has bundled up their dirty sports uniforms and bloodied bed sheets and arranged their kicked-off shoes in neat rows a thousand times over. Has been the beneficiary of their cast-offs, unwanted birthday presents too good to waste—cashmeres in the wrong color, Levi's in the wrong cut. Mothers insisting: *Brand new, with the tags and everything.* As if there might still be room to be embarrassed by charity.

If not these two, then their counterparts. Matti has peered into certain details of their lives, intimate and occasionally unseemly, in a way they will never see into hers. In this she sometimes feels a grave and fleeting superiority, almost pities them their limitations. They might only learn about such lives in books or films, slum tourism, passing through in a matter of pages or hours, then moving on to debate the merit of stories in which women were not strong, did not overcome, women who allowed bad things to happen to them.

She still calculates everything in houses cleaned, tallying them up in her mind's eye like the little plastic Monopoly tokens, the tiny red and green homes and hotels standing in for earnings as much as for her time, the skin on her hands. Suze and Alex will become the kind of people who move the little pieces around the board. Matti will remain the kind of woman who allows things to happen to her, good or bad. Who allows herself to be renamed.

• • •

When she was young she imagined sleep as a shallow tidal pool, first dry then slowly filling, herself at the bottom of it.

Sleep and the ocean, not dissimilar. These vast, unfathomable bodies with shifting borders, which we might slip into, become immersed in, alongside innumerable others of whose presence we are dimly or urgently aware, and whom we might brush up against now and again in a way that is thrilling, or terrible. (All rivers run to the sea. All time, all knowing, all memory. All forgetting, too. All longing.) When sleep will not have her, there is still the water. She may give herself to the ocean in a way she never can now, with sleep.

They reach the west coast in monsoon rain, the ocean slate-gray and heaving. Offshore, an old tanker has cracked open, hemorrhaging its cargo into the sea.

So much for swimming.

The whale sharks have gained a mythic allure over the course of the drive. But so much for whale sharks, too.

The rain has a warm, animal sentience about it, an appetite for skin that will not be dissuaded, nosing about in crevices, under shirt collars, behind earlobes like a persistent lover.

They linger three days in a quagmired caravan park, waiting for the weather to turn, compensating for the malaise with the withered saffron mushrooms Alex crushes to powder and steeps to the tea that Matti at first declines and then accepts.

Just enough to bring the colors up, Suze tells her, the taste still exactly like dirt under the thick of honey.

By the firelight they're stretched out, Suze and Alex, holding each other's ankles, working with upholstery needles and ink from broken ballpoints, inscribing the

Roman numerals for major arcana in the smooth soft place beneath the joint.

Doesn't it hurt? Matti asks from her side of the fire.

Nothing really hurts, says Alex, not lifting her eyes from her work. Pain's a choice we make.

Blue and blood smeared together on her man's shirt cuff, Suze's heel in her palm.

Suze bestows a slow, beatific smile.

It's not too much, Matti. Why, do you want one? she asks.

Knowing, probably, that Matti will shake her head, that she has no understanding of the tarot. Perhaps knowing that the question alone will make her stand and leave her place by the fire, walking alone beyond its reach, beyond sight of van and tent. Deeper into the grounds, to spend an hour or more communing with the silvergreen moths that flock to the walls of the brick shower block. Deciphering the encryptions patterning their wings, the intimate tremblings and subaudible purr of their feathery antennae. Aware that this is language, even if it falls outside her comprehension. That there would be people who could comprehend what it means, who have devoted their lives to comprehending.

There is a change, barely perceptible—a minute shift in temperature or pressure, a slight swing in the direction of the wind, or some other internal, subliminal signal undetected by Mathilde—and in a hyper-percussive stammering of wings, the moth assembly alters orientation, counterclockwise by 90 degrees.

Or maybe it is only the force of her attention that disturbs them, interferes with their signaling. This seems, in the moment, unbearable to her. This and the strip fluorescence of the overhead lighting, unbearable.

She removes herself, venturing deeper into the scrub and the downpour, as far as possible from the lights and the sounds of other human voices, from electricity whining through wires. Her shoes abandoned somewhere, the rain a fine mesh skin. Little lights swim at the corners of her eyes, like tiny curious fish who do not know to be afraid of bigger animals. Again the wet, clinging feeling of forgotten things, fleetingly recovered. Of wading out beyond her depth and at last finding home there, so close, all this time.

She kneels, reverent, in the dirt and throws up, opening her eyes again at dawn, fingers encircling the ropy musculature of an exposed tree root, the thickness of a familiar wrist. *I've loved you all my life*, she wants to say, possibly says.

Must have said, taste of dirty rain there in her mouth.

On the way back to the van she glimpses her reflection in a station wagon window, map of dirt thatched to one cheek. The moth congregation is still fixed, devout, to the outer wall of the shower block. In the light of day they seem inert and unknowing, their radiance muted.

By the time she finds her way to the campsite something has shifted, again, between the others, wordlessly packing wet gear into the van. A coiled, unspoken fury running like a hot wire between them, sleeping bags rolled sloppily with tense arms, shoved into crevices, under seats. Suze plants herself up front, behind the wheel, insisting she has memorized the map. Alex stretches out in back, a damp shirt covering her eyes, leaving Matti to ride shotgun, and as they set out for the Dampier nobody speaks.

In days that follow she'll steal covert glances at the numerals—The Tower (Alex), The Star (Suze)—swelling angrily beneath their wet slicks of paw-paw ointment.

• • •

Good Friday draining out when they turn off the paved road for the Dampier. The dark drawn raucously across the sky by legions of flying foxes, their endless tide of leather and velvet.

Alex has directions, barely decipherable, scrawled by a musterer in Broome. They're supposed to lead to a quiet spot near water, good for camping, walking distance from a painted cave known only to locals.

The road they're traveling does not appear on any of their own maps. A rough track, more of a washout, half lost to erosion and flanked by the craggy upcroppings of termite mounds. They loom knowingly, like neolithic henges, or the remnants of a red-earth acropolis. The even greater industry below, subterranean; crawling catacombs beneath the broken donkey track they're traveling.

Now and again, through the scrub, the van's headlights reveal sheathes of white cotton, striped flannel, plaid: the more human-sized ant nests attired in tattered shirts, cast-off hats, bedsheet capes and skirts. A wedding veil fashioned from a mosquito net.

Matti slows the van to a juddering crawl, and they're engulfed by the acrid reek of the engine overheating.

Fuck's sake, don't slow down. Alex herself now convinced the stationhand's map will more likely lead them to shallow bush graves.

Hold on, Mat—

It's Suze who spots the water tank from the road. And beyond that, standing some way off into the scrub, the curved roof of a horse float, reddened by rust or dirty rain.

We can ask in there.

• • •

On the cusp of the Wet and the Dry, they pull in. The three women spill out of the van in boots, sandals, bare feet, hair stiff with sweat and seawater. Calling in voices loud at first, then hushed as they cross the threshold of the slumped veranda.

No one home.

Reckon fucking not, the roof like that.

Everything's left just so, though. Spooky.

Maybe they carked it out there somewhere. Or in here.

Oh Christ, do not.

The water doesn't run . . .

What'd you expect, iced tea and pikelets?

No shower, no shitter . . .

A boot goes through a soft place in the floor. A yelp and then laughter. They tread tentative through each of the rooms, surveying. Evidence of a life, a man's life, lived solo and now furred under years of dust and bird grime. No one is coming back here, whether or not he ever meant to. A clay bowl upturned on the basin, shaving brush bristles caked with hardened soap.

In the bedroom a bookcase, and a simple cupboard for clothes. An olive wool overcoat that Matti shakes and holds against herself. She brings a sleeve to her nose: dogs and sweat and smoke. Shreds of rolling tobacco and cigarette papers still there in the pockets.

Anyway, she says, I'm keeping this.

But Suze and Alex are elsewhere in the house, busy pulling drawers open, ransacking cupboards

There's a bed, but a person would be cracked to sleep on it—iron frame, still tucked drum tight in mercenary wool, the covered mattress probably home to innumerable invisible lifeforms, microbes and arthropods, spores from maladies all but written out of history. The ceiling is crumbling away in the cornice above, admitting a long funnel of black mold that has crept down over time and is now colonizing the floorboards.

The books in the case are mostly manuals, and mostly eaten through, rewritten by silverfish. Texts on marine engines and whale species and fungi and icebergs. An old shop ledger filled with cross-sectioned diagrams of termite mounds, fastidious annotations and coordinates, unanswered questions hovering in the margins. Glossaries of Pacific Island languages and customs, games played by children—*catching dragonflies with a woman's hair tied between two small stones.* Copies of National Geographic,

Antarctic Journal. Something called *The Observer's Handbook*, ordered by subscription from the Royal Astronomical Society of Canada and mailed care of the post office in Broome. Star maps of the wrong skies, names and visitational frequencies of comets. Venus at perihelion. The moons have little faces, their expressions all doleful, no matter which phase they signify—gloomy in both waxing and waning profiles, gloomier still full-face.

Otherwise, a few tattered Russian behemoths, and a slim leather-bound collection of poems, Yeats, heavily underlined.

And moth-like stars were flickering out

She pockets the Yeats, closes the door on that room.

The kitchen, stone-floored, seems spared. Almost habitable. A heavy table with its two chairs filling most of the space, a fireplace and a long wooden box pushed against one wall. The box is filled with boughs of some kind, broad flat tropical leaves none of them recognize— good for kindling maybe—and beneath that, dry packing straw, no doubt housing generations of redbacks. They shut the lid and drag it closer to the table for a bench.

In the center of the table they heap their loot—candles and citronella, beautiful tools, a bottle of brown liquor, still sealed with red wax. A stockpile of promising jars and tins, labeled and not. Tea and sugar stored matryoshka style, jar within another jar to protect against insect invasion.

Don't make this anymore, do they? Alex holds up a tin of malt syrup, pries off the buckled lid, but inside it's something different, a resinous yellow-white powder with a faintly chemical reek.

They burn the candles and citronella to ward off the darkness and bloodsuckers. Empty jars and chipped mugs are wiped of dust to hold liquor, and they dare each other through the nameless brown firewater that might be brandy, or anything. They skol and tear up, sinuses burning, coughing up fresh invectives like filthy treasure, words Matti had forgotten she knew.

Suze, inspired, goes out to the van to ferret out a tin of condensed milk, improvising what she calls Randy Alexandras. In honor of. Shaking them up in a mason jar, thickly sweet and steadily sickening. The night grows similarly cloying, and close, the world beyond melting away into black nothingness at the edge of the candlelight. An oblivion that Matti wants to melt into, also, but the others beat her to it—*Back in a tick, mate*—disappearing to smoke or fuck under the endless moth-like stars, amid the termitaria.

Matti puts her head on the table. After a while, the van's doors slam closed. Then the crackle of the radio, a song she doesn't know. She was right, they've forgotten her.

She is tired, anyway, of the airless nights in the van. Buggered of guy ropes and tent pitching. Tired of overhearing their whisper-hissed pillow talk, tired of their trust-funded rebellions, their matching home-inked tarot tatts.

She makes space for herself there, on the stone floor of the stranger's kitchen, pushing the box back to its place by the wall and spreading his green coat on the flagstones by the hearth. The landlord, she could call him. She upends the dregs of the brandy into her mug and fishes the cigarette makings out of his coat pocket. Tries rolling a smoke but the tobacco crumbles straight to dust and the endeavor falls apart.

Sleep comes for her, at last, on the flag floor of the dilapidated house, and with it the river. In sleep she wades deeper into the alluvial silt of those old dreams, slipping out into the dark, past the other pregnant cast-outs, past the sleeping horses to the river.

Even at seventeen, she'd held no romantic illusions about purity. The river's current carried detritus, visible and not: household rubbish, stormwater-borne effluent, the carcasses of unlucky marsupials and rodents and birds, engine oil and the toxic runoff from factories, muck from slaughterhouses and illegal septic systems, and God knew what else.

But it fed life, all the same: trees snaked their roots into it, animals came to drink, yabbies whistled silver from their muddy burrows. It could keep her, too. It could bear her off, aloft. Somewhere. Who said water had no memory.

She wakes cold, clenched, the nighttime temperature at nadir, the day's heat vanished, crept out from the stones. Rancid taste in her mouth from Suze's brandy concoction, and a hollow knock behind her sternum, the grief-ache of something missing, taken.

She remembers Suze and Alex, off together in the van—but no, not them. It's Sally, she realizes. Sally whose limbs she ought to have woken to, woven through, out of that particular dream (the thickness of a familiar wrist). Sally or the boy; now as then, the losses are not divisible. One grief rousts another, restless siblings turning over in a too-small bed.

Outside, a clear dark night of no moon, the stars more like apertures than celestial bodies, pinhole portals to an icy-bright elsewhere. The last candles smothered, wicks drowned in their own wax.

So make a fire, you sook. (Sally's voice, or how she remembers Sally's voice.)

She pulls the coat around herself and squats on her heels before the woodbox, lifting out the broad-leaved boughs, banging each one methodically against the side to dislodge whatever might be nesting there.

She piles up the kindling in the hearth, unsure of how it will burn, adding fistfuls of the packing straw for tinder. The stalks flare up briefly, bright, their oily leaves sparking and giving up a resinous smoke, but the wood is slow to catch. The darkness presses back. She flings in more fistfuls of the straw, primed to be bitten and too cold to care. The light in the room blooms and recedes, a slow pulse that she tends, the heat and color only momentary, as a memory partially recalled. She keeps going, until the layer of dry grass gives way to fabric, her fingers grazing stiff silk, a rumpled sleeve that tapers to a small papery hand knuckled in a tight fist around a string of rosary beads, clay or bone or coral.

She has seen saints before—in paintings, etchings, in the photographs of encyclopedias and trash-and-treasure postcards, their scalloped edges and surreal tints, souvenired from reliquaries throughout Europe and sent back to some Aunt Jeannie or Pru in Boronia or Black Rock.

Never in life. Never in her life.

The small sharp knuckles, clamped around the rosary, threaten to puncture the skin. There is no air of peace in it.

Mathilde sweeps away the last of the straw, moved beyond herself, beyond fear or repulsion. When she uncovers the girl's face, masked by chaff and dust, it's not horror she feels. A dreadful wonder. Or not wonder—the awe and the wrongness of it.

She looks. Then brings her face close to the child's and blows to lift the grit from the dark lashes, the way she once saw somebody do with a toddler at the beach, their eyes inflamed by sand.

The lids are not quite closed. They remain that way, unmoving. No flicker or gleam behind them.

The girl's lips, too, are parted over small teeth, slightly spaced.

An understanding that blooms in Mathilde, without words, of Thirst. Or a longing with the nature of Thirst.

There is no obvious sign of injury. Maybe a wound, hidden out of sight under the layers, dressed and packed with whatever hallowed material was appropriate to saints. Rare herbs, ermine fur, swans' down? She has no idea, and no inclination to discover.

When the fire dips, she feeds it Yeats, the scrawled-over end pages and then the works themselves.

The costume the girl is laid out in, the silk and ruffles and tiers of heavy beading, aren't for living in, let alone playing in, that much is obvious. All that adornment must have come after—after *what?*—for appearance's sake. For display. To be looked upon, revered. Entreated, as the girls at the Home did of Saint Hildegard.

But for what? When so young.

And why here, with this man, no holy books among his disintegrating science manuals. Only the poems, which speak heterodoxically of God, but in any case keep the fire going.

But something rustled on the floor,
And some one called me by my name.

Pearl divers might have brought her here, a century ago, from wherever they'd come. Or miners, during the rush, for luck. A child-sized rabbit's foot.

In glimpses of how her own life might have swiveled, been turned on its incomprehensible axis or profoundly broken open by chance or desire or weakness or luck, of course this was never. This was never how.

There is something to be done, but she can't yet imagine what.

She knows only that it is for her alone to right something. And also that it is far too late for right.

At a loss—with the light burnt down and the fuel torn up—she covers the girl's face with the splayed book boards before gently replacing the leaves and unburnt boughs, and lowering the lid. Sweeping up the scattered leaves and seedpods, she's uncertain whether the debris itself is made holy, by proximity. She cups the matter in her hands a moment. Then, deferring, adds it to the coat pocket with the stale rolling tobacco.

The morning is cool and gray and shadowless. Silence from the van, and from the termite mounds, incubating, their rough warmth under her palms as she grazes them in passing. Beyond them, past the contorted armature of what was once a greenhouse, the white horse float rests at a tilt, backed into the scrub and stained with eucalypt tannin and weather, its hitch bedded in the red dirt.

Inside the float there is nothing: no tack, no gear. Just a scatter of wind-borne dust and dried leaves.

• • •

She wakes late in the stranger's house, to sun glaring through the grimy kitchen window, camp-stove cooking noises from outside. Her body slow to respond, ankle and hip bones clicking as she gets herself upright.

Alex is beside the van, brewing up the last of the coffee. Adding *coffee* to a list of things that need replacing: *condensed milk, bread, eggs, meds, chips, vodka, jam, Golds*.

Matti wordlessly fills her cup, still sticky at the rim. Suze is out among the termite mounds, collecting auras.

Framing up a monolith in the viewfinder, a few yards from the water tank. The caps of her shoulders gleam like oiled wood through the slit sleeves of her shirt, her legs and feet bare.

Morning, Sunflower, she says from behind the camera. Well, almost afternoon now. We didn't want to wake you—dead to the world when we looked in. But you must've needed it, hey. Did you manage to dream?

No.

Finally Suze clicks the shutter, and a square tongue of film emerges with a grinding mechanical whirr.

She extracts the Polaroid and turns. Too bad, you looked like you were dreaming.

Matti swallows coffee, unsettled by being observed in sleep.

Far beyond unwilling, she will not be capable of telling them, either of them, what she has seen. Afraid now that if she even speaks, some hint of it will be there, of secrecy, and Suze will know to press for more.

Feels charged here, right? Suze says, fanning the Polaroid under her chin. Not in a hairy way, but, I don't know. Big. Anyway, we were thinking it might be good to dig in for a while. A few days, a week maybe. Re-ground ourselves a bit, you know, actually connect? All this moving, tearing through. It's not really natural. Like we're being chased—who's chasing us?

She waits, still fanning the photograph. So, what about you . . . Would you mind?

What is clear to Matti is that the two of them—Alex and Suze—are fused, sheltered together in the "we."

What is not clear is whether they mean for her to stay on with them, alongside, a kind of mascot-witness, or whether they would prefer (*would she mind*) if she traveled on separately from here. A bus, or a second-class ticket on the train. (How many houses, cleaned, would that work out to?)

I don't mind, she says. Either way. Then, not allowing for the possibility of exile: I'm happy to stay.

Suze's face is a warm, benevolent mask, half hidden by the shade of her hat brim.

You sure? Don't want to mess things up with your work or anything.

Matti shakes her head. It isn't pride that keeps her from admitting that she has nothing to go back to. Her own dread of the fact, perhaps, the floorlessness of it. A deep open-water feeling, almost thrilling.

All right, Suze says. Well. I'm glad you're here with us. She squints at the sky. We were thinking about heading back into town for a restock, if we're staying on. Alex was making a list. Back by dark, I reckon.

You remember the way?

We'll figure it out. Want us to grab you anything?

I'll just come along.

Righto. I'll go let 'lex know. Suze raises the camera again, but Mathilde turns away. Suze sighs and lets the camera dangle from its strap.

Here, she says, holding out the earlier Polaroid. See what manifests for you.

The image of the ant mound steadily gaining definition and vibrancy. Mathilde knows what she is supposed to do, Suze's method for manifestation. Press her hot fingers around its outline, manipulating the chemicals before they set.

Mathilde holds the photograph at the outer edges. Allows the image to fix, just as it is.

• • •

Suze moves like honey down the supermarket aisles, camera strap biting into her brown shoulder. Hot dirty feet on the cool dirty lino. Weet-Bix and brown rice and peanut butter, coffee and chocolate and mangoes and meds. The shelf stackers eyeing Suze, her bikini bottoms and her dark areolae visible through the thin stuff of her shirt dress.

Suze squints at the list. Did Alex mean tinned tomatoes or fresh?

No idea, Matti says.

The fresh ones look sad.

I can go ask.

Tell her the fresh ones looks woeful. And ask if she's actually for real about us finding basil here.

Out front, Alex leans in the phone booth with its kicked-in glass, negotiating with her parents at the far end of the line. Mathilde stands out of earshot and raises a hand. Alex looks directly at her but makes no sign of having seen.

If she could be either of them, she realizes, she would be Alex.

At the van she wonders whether to unload their belongings. No.

She keeps to the speed limit while driving through town, and once at the outskirts guns the engine, late sun catching the dusty impressions Suze's feet have left on the windscreen.

How many hours will be needed? To hitch the float, freight it up, reach the coast?

She tears back along the stationhand's road, propelled by a dread that something will have happened, that someone will have come while she's been gone. After so many years? But yes, an urgency that won't be reasoned with, every corrugation and hitch traveling through the steering wheel and up her arms, every pothole threatening to rip the chassis out from underneath her. The smooth backs of submerged boulders the sleek humps of great stone whales breaching the dusty surface. She swerves for something possum-sized; the tires lose traction and the van skids hard to the shoulder, leaves slapping through the open window.

She corrects the wheel and forces herself to slow, to suck the dusty air deep into her lungs and hold it there. Useless if she writes it off now. And nobody has come, in all this time. In however many years. And nobody is chasing after her, now. In any case it wouldn't occur to them to come back this way. They would see no reason for her to return to the house alone. Would recall nothing of particular value.

• • •

They may still call the cops. In spite of all their railing against the system.

She wonders how she will explain it to them. If she ever sees them again.

It doesn't figure now. They have money, and parents who will wire them more. They have hotels and airfares and new clothes if they want them, they can go back to Melbourne or they can travel on north.

All roads remain open to them.

Her foot settles back into the accelerator pedal.

For Mathilde there is only this one road: red, unsealed, rutted and eroding between the rocky protrusions of antworks, beginning and ending beyond her knowing, though it is imminently clear to her that she has been traveling toward it her whole life.

The divot that overturns the van is nothing much.

There is time to wonder: *For this?* as the van swings out wide from the pinion of the steering wheel and then back, loose stones and dirt flowing beneath the locked tires like poured grain. When she tips off the road's shoulder and rolls, the light within the van is almost subaquatic; the inert inland water of yabbie dams and rain-fed seasonal lakes, emulsive and crowded with matter.

Time does not slow, it simply heaps up, unspooling into this small space and holding in suspension all the airborne particles and incidental atomic concretions that amount to shoes and cigarette lighters and sunscreen bottles, the enclosed murmuration of camping gear and scattered loose change, the scissor jack tumbling lazily as a satellite toward the windscreen, brief trajectories that go unwitnessed by the driver (whose eyes, for the most part, are clenched shut) although various configurations will play out for the rest of her life, whenever she returns to marveling at how it was, how it was that the full jerrican of petrol jettisoned from the far back of the van up to the front merely clipped her temple before shattering the windscreen, or how in the hail shower of glass that followed she was left with no cuts, no abrasions. Though her mouth filled with the taste of iron, and the taint of petrol and dirty sugar—Suze's Chanel bottle busted open somewhere.

The van completes two revolutions, or three, she'll never be certain, and hovers at the cusp of another before crunching to a spent tilt against an ancient lightning-struck silver gum. Leaning the way an animal might, into the warmth of a hip or a hand, passenger-side tires pawing on air. At some point the wipers have come on, a plaintive mewling, while the radio crackles through a commercial. She cuts the ignition. Waits for flames, for pain to announce itself through the baffle of shock.

The silvered bark of the tree, close enough to rest her cheek against, and scrawled over with the calligraphy of borers that reads like Nazca lines, signals to other, extraterrestrial life.

She deciphers them perfectly. This, now, is Act Three.

Mathilde places her palm against the rough hide of the old eucalypt, pushes until her shoulder burns and the van responds, crunching back onto all fours.

When she tries the ignition, the engine turns over. As if nothing.

Through the shattered windscreen, the dull gleam of the water tank beyond the trees. The rain-dirty roof of the horse float.

Many years from prayer, sincere or enforced, Mathilde calls upon the graces to hand:

The tremble of the gearshift beneath her palm.

The name she gave to a child, not spoken aloud in eighteen years.

Her wakefulness. Her Hunger.

Float

The horse float, again. *Sin caballos*. She would of course prefer if there were horses.

The jolting antwork road. By night, this time, new moon blacked out by the earth. No difference. What she knows of the immediate, the imminent world is not divided into

lit /

unlit

though her awareness reaches only a little way beyond herself, a lamp swung into the dark: the labyrinthine catacombs and chemical communing of the termite colonies below, the buckled van hauling the float south, the white grip and burning intent of the woman with her hands on the wheel, humming something, the words and the images that swash beneath the humming.

• • •

The canoe-wood box shifts on the wooden floor of the trailer. She shifts, is shifted within the box, rolling this way and back with each bend, half the packing gone.

The men who'd first carted her out this way, into this ant-eaten country a quarter century ago, had no inkling and little interest in what they carried. Imagined tools, or horse tack, and drove accordingly, with no mind to the comfort of the freight.

Well, nothing hurts, anyway.
Still, something like dignity. Something like self-regard.

The men spoke of razor blades and women and rabbit trapping, and of a great wave that had come once and would again, surging deep inland toward the heart of the country and drinking up everything in its path. Islands made of mountaintops, and all that lay below these mountain-islands drowned.

She held on to a few of their words (habit).
She held on to the promise of the wave.

She could wait.

• • •

The woman goes more carefully. Aware, more or less, of what she carries. Whom. Of the two of them, the woman understands herself to be the younger. Possibly by centuries. Imagines that this girl-sized, unwaking wonder may still be capable of knowing discomfort (not exactly), susceptible to injury or at least breakage (possible, not known).

The urgency that moves her she now calls by other names, attributes to higher influence. Not fear or panic but Intervention. Providence. She stops the van only once, pulling off into the scrub to knock the remaining shivers of broken glass out of the windscreen's frame. Her hair blown wild, wiry, almost possum colored. Though not old. Young enough to think herself old, oblivious to just how much life there will be left to make use of, to invent meaning and purpose for. Her body taut with self-denial, soft in secret places with want, her mind burning on its own Hunger, eating itself up like a black star. She burns on through the new-moon dark, every so often dipping her head to the mirror, or twisting her neck to check the float, dimly bathed in red twilight glow. The Pleiades dangling overhead, out of reach of the inverted Archer.

• • •

Stars. Little more known of stars.

Little known of the destination, beyond what can be gleaned, unbraided from this woman's mind. More might be known if the mind in question were not so much like a lead ocean under a closed sky viewed through warped and salt-streaked glass. Obscured, kept secret from itself.

Huge dark shapes sliding around beneath the surface, left nameless and unstoried, so that even she, miraculous or otherwise, cannot tell what those others might be. Even brushing up against them, herself only another dark shape shifting beneath the surface.

(If the woman feels her there, nosing around. She does not push back.)

They follow the coast. South, the way each of them came here by, a day ago, a quarter century ago, no difference. They will follow this road until the woman is told—believes she is told—*Here*.

What makes the living suppose they are of any use whatever to the dead? Or the dead to them, for that matter? That there are answers on this side that might be haggled or pestered for.

Death has brought very little in the way of answers. At least so far. Only more aggravating questions.

Granted, her situation is not what anyone could call ordinary.
    Not death in the usual sense, in keeping with the natural order of things. Only time breaking contract with her body.

Perhaps the real dead know more.

Perhaps she belongs, for now, as much to the living, her former place among them, her people.

Her People. She has outlived them all. In a sense. Her being, or much of its housing; her composite molecular self still recognizable, not yet entirely rent apart. While her family—that unified sensate stuff that was her sister, her sister's child—have slipped back into the All. Rain into stream, stream into river, on into ocean, however it's supposed to go. She is distantly aware of their Elsewhereness. Or, their no-longer-Hereness, their being beyond all immediate reach.

They did not pass her by, on their way to this otherness, wherever it was. Or not in any form she could recognize.

To miss them is to miss the point. To miss at all—this is the idiot anguish, the small stupid sorrow of the self.

To know this, and still to have edges that refuse to give. Hard and soft tissues resistant, clinging to the known form, maintaining a boundary between self and All. Even if her body was—was and remains, if now to a lonelier extent—a plurality, a midget universe unto itself, grounding place to a vast assembly of inhabitants (microflora, archaea, viruses, fungi, bacteria), certain of which have long since taken their leave. Abandoned, rats off a ship. A virus, to be fair, having limited prospects for contagion here. While others have remained, seemingly having no need or desire for new or broader horizons.

Tempting to imagine something like loyalty. Affinity, even.

What are the rules, and who makes them? This knowledge, no closer.
In any case, her name is no longer spoken.

And what of the first, the former life, now? What of the irresistible, verdantly sordid vocabularies of port and canal and street workers, reverberated by parrots sold in cages throughout Casco Viejo, music till dawn and the crisp easy pockets of sunburnt cruise passengers, the afternoon rains that clung and still cling in drenching sticky veils, strung across the isthmus, between Pacific and Caribbean, over City and Jungle? What of cold honeycomb, and bright oil, and hurt dog, and how long, how long since she has felt rain on her face? Her own careful cache of echoes and afterimages saved from that time confused and crowded out, subsumed by the clattering inner workings and ramblings of others, their forlorn implorings, obsessions, adorations, their resentments and sentiments, memories real and invented, dreams, fantasies, visions fixed as vivid and engulfing as the instant of first experience (*I only came cause you called out*), the long afterlight of the obliterated incident too loud too large too much to be contained within such small and shallow-bodied hosts.

• • •

All push in, uninvited, snaking over the remnants of selfhood like arrowhead creeper, rampant and indiscriminate, steadily enveloping whatever might be left of her own life, such as it was, and whatever she loved in the time that she had there. Her carefully concealed inner reliquary.

(When she was young—*young?*—before time broke contract with her body, and the earth refused to eat her, she had often wished to read minds. Imagined it useful, a quiet door to power. The reality is much more tedious, and exhausting. And usually of little fascination or surprise—a never-ending torrent, a radio that can't simply be switched off or thrown out of a window, visitors who won't leave and in the meantime refuse to shut up.)

They follow the coast. She is aware that outside the metal hull of the float, the night air is damp, would feel chill upon the sweat slicking the woman's skin, would cause her bare arms to prickle with gooseflesh.

The woman herself does not notice, makes no attempt to get warm, to drag a shirt from somewhere in the upended confusion of belongings.

(Gooseflesh. Chicken skin, piel de gallina.
Bird skin, thorn pricks, porcupinefish, ant tits.
No accounting for it, then or now.)

What is hers and what is not? Sunlight welling like warm oil in the open palm of an outflung hand, the day's sunbaked groundheat soaking up into the knuckles, pressed like that between earth and sky, held on the luscious cusp of sleep. Smell of new grass, running sap. Kiss behind ear. Kiss behind knee. Kiss on mouth that buzzes, rings in teeth. Frisson, the sudden rush of one's own innate alchemy being instantaneously rearranged by another's. Fresh hungers. Flavors impossible to have ever actually tasted, lurid and curious fruit never so much as seen or imagined in life. In her own life. Scenes she could not have witnessed. Voices and music unknown.

This much, death, this approximation of death, has granted. Though it is really not so much of a consolation, after all:

The ability to reach into the mind of another, a little farther than she once could.

Again, not as far as might be hoped. And not always, often not, at her discretion.

And besides this?

If she were asked, and were able to provide an answer in words, she might choose:

Death brought one closer to ants.

Meaning only: ants, us, gods. No difference.

Huntsman magpie birchbark brittlestar carpart limpet stalactite stone . . . No difference.

Or the difference so temporary, so fleeting, it does not matter.

If this was the lesson, surely she didn't need to die, or not like that, in order to come to it.

Surely she could have found her own way to it, given a little more time.

Is this what holds her here? This pining for the far off, the fading life.
Or simply a failing of entropy.
No higher design. Just a random, freakish stranding.
They follow the coast. The woman's face is sharp with listening. She is listening the way, receiving the way, the night too dark for otherwise. Eyes strained beyond the weak reach of the remaining headlight and the torrent of winged things that hurtle out of the void into its beam and on through the missing windscreen to amass in the interior, battering hectically until being swept back out into oblivion. The bright beaded net of stars overhead, unreadable but for the Cross, the Archer, the cluster of Sisters forever just out of his reach. Forever but only just.

• • •

Some hours from now, at a point the woman believes *safe* (the fuel gauge deep in the red, as it has been for many kilometers), she will at last turn the wheel toward the water.

She will be weeping, as she opens the box. Weeping as she removes the remaining branches and packing to uncover the small, clenched hands, the fierce, unsleeping face, gathering the gaudily costumed bundle into her arms and lifting carefully, as though not wanting to shock into wakefulness. Any child carried from any vehicle after a long journey. The weight across her forearms, against her chest, no heavier than the coat carried out of the stranger's house, the girl seeming hollow-boned as a bird beneath all the layers of crepe and beading, empty as a whelk shell emptied of whelk. The sound of something unseen within, tinking as if loose. The small sleek head of dark tight-braided hair tucked under her chin, secure.

The hair smells of beeswax, of cut hay and smoke, sweet almond oil, desiccated flowers and once-green things crushed to dust, water under shade. And something further beneath that again, denser, sweeter, richer; this side of life but more secret.

The woman cries harder, heaves with crying.

What have you got to howl about? If words, the formation of words were still possible, the lips and lungs and vocal folds responsive . . .

What the fuck have you got . . .

But then she might just as likely raise her arms. Reach for the damp dusty neck, be complicit in her carrying.

Relics—you could call them that—drop onto the sand, no longer of meaning, if they were ever. Embroidered slippers that have never been stood up in, whose soles have never touched earth, falling one after the other onto the beach as if kicked. The whittled red beads of the coral rosary, returned to their kind.

• • •

The woman, done with weeping now, the rocks underfoot whiskery with seagrass, or studded with sharp colonies of mollusks, eyes open and closed. Tidal pools brimming with other life (voices and music unknown).

The woman never looking down, planting each foot with the weight of her certainty, and so sure-footedly lacerating them on shattered coral, oyster shells, the busted hulls of crustacea, which is only to be expected, only in keeping with circumstance, the conveyance of yet another child to yet another future that will not contain her.
    I am (she thinks, bloodily) a conduit.
    That is all.

The tide will be wrenching, on the outward. They will go on, out to meet it, to where waves break against the reef beds and the ocean drops away, begins. The current drawing hungrily on the drenched confection of froth and frills. Saltwater lapping at parchment skin.

Will she go just like sugar? The woman, treading water now, snarled up in the heavy wet netting of silk and lace, the drenchweight dragging the two of them out, beyond grasp of the reef, into the dream she has had all her life.

The water will press in, against the frail seal of eyelids and lips, rushing past the small teeth and flooding the speechless mouth with brine, spilling on into airways, down the long-dormant corridors of arteries, fallow passageways, to reach the dry hollows of lungs and stomach, the empty ventricles of the silent, fist-sized muscle

the ocean like a great hand opening inside her
her own hands unclenching in response

III

Bunker

The quiet had left me. That's how I put it, but I meant Maree. Most of her cosmetics abandoned in a swollen-stuck bathroom drawer. Hydrators, anti-aging, *complexion correction*. Potions, I called them, like an old man describing a woman's things. A few days after she left I tried them on myself, mostly for the smell of her. Of course they did not correct anything, did not make me more beautiful, only streaked me to an unconvincing shade, Maree's, darker and more lustrous than my own. I accepted why she'd gone. She'd made a choice, and it wasn't the wrong choice. Her folks old and susceptible, too proud to see it and too stubborn to budge. Bad reception where they are. Have to climb a hill to make a call. But she never climbs the bloody hill.

And her emails, when they do come, arrive in business hours.

There are people in the world who've never thrown a plate at a wall. Think of that.

Evenings when the phone rings out and out and I think I'll never drag in a full breath again I put my feet into Maree's boots and I take the dog to check on Tilde's. Though Tilde is gone now, too. Until February she'd been our closest neighbor. Now she's up at St. Elisabeth's, where nobody but family can get at her, and she has no family that we know of.

In town I'd heard from Thorpe at the Ampol about how Tilde was when they took her to St. E's, how she'd been found idling in front of the diesel bowser in the morning dark, reciting something, barely dressed despite the frost and running a temperature of 41 degrees.

Reciting what, I wanted to know. We stood the regulation distance apart, Thorpe in his year-round uniform of khaki coveralls.

Usual gibberish, he said, not unkindly. But in spite of all that and what with the nightie and no shoes, she was quite plausible, really quite plausible . . .

I didn't know what he meant by plausible—genial? Agreeable? Comprehensible? Coherent? In any case, I felt guilty for not getting to her first, before it came to all that.

You're not responsible for her, Syb, Thorpe said. She's been seeing after herself out there since before you were a glint.

He was letting us off the hook, Maree and me. But in a way we were, responsible, obliged by proximity if nothing else, even if we haven't known her as long as some.

I thought—still think—of the two ancient, adjacent neighbors I had, the year I lived in a colossal city. Six floors up, and no lift. Each morning one would shuffle along the landing to the door of the other, knocking and calling out: *Still alive in there?* or *Are you dead yet, my friend?*

Not yet, Pussycat. How 'bout you?

Fairly certain Tilde isn't dead yet. Someone would surely say. Then Maree would have a reason to pick up her damn phone.

Three ks to Tilde's, and the sky looks poisoned. I let the dog go when we reach the catchment, and she bolts down into the dry basin of the reservoir. Dry six years, and baked hard as a French tennis court, fissured with cracks. The water gauge stranded center-left, impossible numbers scored at intervals, indicating depths that are unthinkable now, already.

If you see me, weep.

That's what's written—etched, I think—onto stones in a riverbed somewhere in Europe. A message from a hundred years ago that reappears in times of drought.

These are the kinds of things Tilde knows and likes to talk about. And this is what I think of when I see the lowest depth marks, the murky zero and then the rusty nothing at the bottom of the gauge.

Really it says, in flaking blue paint: *If ya ever this dry call Alannah.*

It's a town of barely five hundred, and if there was an Alannah, we'd know about her. Otherwise I might—dial the numbers, or what's left of them.

I stay up at the rim, watching the dog zigzag below, pawing at the ashy hollows of charred eucalypts that have tumbled down since the last fires. The dry basin still teeming with dog beauty, as Maree calls it, her term for certain qualities all but lost on human senses and aesthetics. But we've begun to have eyes for it, or so we like to think.

The dog runs back up the embankment, weaving between my legs, lovingly jeopardizing me. A gorgeous animal—red-gold with fennec-like ears, and as always it feels radiant to be the subject of her attention. We put on speed over the bare red bull ant fields, so the jumpers don't have time to get purchase, and we keep up that pace until Tilde's forest comes into view; a grove started from a handful of seeds, tipped out of a secondhand coat pocket decades ago, with no notion of what they were. A kind that oughtn't usually grow here, it turned out. Canoe timber, so far inland, coaxed from this clay-clotted soil.

She'd raised them to cover a three-acre plot with all the density of a plantation. Now they towered, blotted the sky. Or sheltered you from it, as you like. The world had gone to the knackery, Tilde said, but she was making her own climate out here. Actually, what she said was: *Fuck 'em, Grow my own fucking air.*

Amid the trees, a clearing, and the train carriage she had for a home.

Rooms too small to haunt, you'd think. But of course no place is too small.

This used to be the kind of place that people sought out, removed to, in order to Prepare. A place others have never left, never had the means to leave. That's how it goes, world over.

Flat-earthers, doomsday prophets, climate migrants. All moved by some tidy compulsion to see out the end of the world from the end of the world.

Tilde has lived a long time here on stewed apples and champagne. What she calls champagne, which is neither the real French stuff nor supermarket sparkling, but a kind of home-stilled ginger vermouth spritzed with Schweppes.

By the time Maree and I met her, she was in her eighties, and although much of her verbal communication came in the form of poems learnt by rote—*Twenty centuries of stony sleep*, and so on—she could still chop a cord of firewood, care for the trees, keep herself and her carriage-home together.

We've come by often since she was taken away, dog and I. To let the air in, keep the dust stirred up. Free the quoll who'd made his own mysterious way in. Browse the spines of her books.

There are people who can read centuries of history in the earwax of whales. How this brief quietening of the world's oceans will be recorded in layers of keratin and fat, lodged in the skulls of Earth's largest mammals. Tilde was maybe never one of these people exactly but she subscribes to these kinds of magazines. Maree had what she called *illuminary* conversations with Tilde. (I made as though not to care too much if our own conversations were less than luminous.) We came to visit her as a pair just the once, and it was obvious Tilde was funny about lesbians. A shame, I said, because she would've made such a good one.

We looked in on her separately, after that. Two, three times a week, taking turns. She never thanked you for it but she was civil. Sat you down at her table and fixed you up with a mug of something instant, then magpie-eye you across the plastic gingham tablecloth—the carnival glass bowl filled with pill packets, matchbooks from dead motels, paper straws of sugar, powdered whitener, salt-and-pepper sachets filched from servos and fast-food joints she'd wander in and out of, stuffing her pockets.

War effort, she called it. And I didn't know if she meant now, or a habit formed in the wake of some previous war, cultivated over a lifetime. Either way, a diligence you had to admire.

There were those in the town who remembered when she arrived, turning up in a battered van at the end of the seventies. Thorpe was one of them, son and apprentice to the town's one mechanic (a distinction he would eventually inherit) and in that way you got a look into just about everyone, sooner or later.

∙ ∙ ∙

He was there the day Tilde's van limped in on its rims, towing an empty horse float.

The float looked sound, but the van was another story, the windscreen missing along with the license plates, every tank on it driven dry.

A wonder it had got her this far, but it would be taking the piss to push it much farther, as Thorpe recalled it.

Firetrap, love—that was his father's professional assessment. Scrap it, or put it up on blocks and grow tomatoes out of it, just don't drive the poor frigging thing another klick.

The horse float had some life in it, though. Could've got a few bob for that, if she'd wanted, plenty of horsey people around then. But that wasn't up for discussion, apparently. It's not like she had six white ponies to cart around, so who knows why.

You got to stop wondering at Tilde's decisions pretty quick. Tilde just did Tilde, right from go.

She was all but shoeless, her ragged tennies stained red by desert dirt, with not much to say about where she'd blown in from and what had brought her here, but she wasn't the first and she wouldn't be the last to come by way of accident or last resort. Plenty of others had arrived in the clothes they stood up in, women alone or with a child clinging to each hand. The town knew weirder: deposed cult leaders, narcoleptic horse trainers, forensic healers and mushroom whisperers, retired crime matriarchs, motocross legends turned infomercial royalty, old cops and old robbers sharing a fence, and while it gossiped and curtain-twitched as much as the next small town, the talk rarely made it across the river.

The Lyddie's full of rumors that couldn't swim, as Thorpe puts it.

At the end of the day, the town was as protective of its fugitives as it was of its runaway wives, and Tilde could have just as easily been either, or both.

No one could say exactly what Tilde's line of living had been, then or ever. She arranged something for that plot of bushland, no services, a fair hike from town and completely off-grid. There was the dam, of course, and in those days at least the dam knew what it was. But no dwelling of any sort, and not many eyes, either. How she preferred it.

She hooked up a generator and installed a couple of rain tanks and rigged some sort of improv irrigation system, and according to Thorpe trees weren't the only thing she was growing out there.

Not that he was one to judge, or cast stones. Why go wasting an aptitude, if you'd clearly been given one?

Tilde accumulated a life out there, piece by piece, living first out of the battered van, then a twelve-foot Millard, and finally the train carriage, a decommissioned Red Rattler brought in by low-loader.

All wheeled things with their miles behind them, observed Thorpe, all of them seen whatever momentum they were ever likely to. Same as Tilde herself, it seemed to him then and so it proved out, a self-fulfilling prophecy.

She was never leaving, come hell or high water. No horses ever materialized, and in fact right near the start of things, in the early eighties with the news full of nukes, she'd buried that old horse float for a bunker.

There was no easy way down into it, but you could tell its whereabouts. The grass having grown back thicker there to carpet it, plush for these parts.

The dog seeks it out, each time we visit. Prostrates herself in the green pile, panting happily.

Maree reckons that if Tilde ever does sleep, she must manage it standing up, like a horse. Maybe fully dressed and open-eyed, a cowboy in an old Western. It's not something either of us has ever caught her at. You might go out at 3 a.m. to stalk off a bad dream or an argument or just to shake some dark spell, and a light would be burning through the trees, the carriage glowing like an oversized Christmas ornament, and no chance she'd be wasting the genny just for a nightlight. All the blinds would be up and she'd either be straight-backed at the kitchen table or upright and in motion, a shadow flowing back and forth across the lit row of windows, poring over one of those magazines, her mind drip-fed by subscription.

You could even knock, at that hour, and Tilde would answer, fully dressed and unsurprised. She wouldn't ask what time you called it, or what the hell you were doing, wandering alone through the belly of the night. She just clocked you with a look that said, *Takes one to know one*, and held the door open wider for you to step in.

Do you know how many kinds of green there are out there? she asked once, as I was fumbling with my headlamp and muddied boots.

She was speaking, as she sometimes would, as if I were a bit thick, but there might yet be hope.

I looked back over my shoulder through the open door. It was a moonless pitch black out there.

Hard to count at this hour, I said.

You couldn't count them at any hour. I've tried keeping a list, but they just keep coming. And we have a sharper eye for green than anything else. Atavism, they'll tell you, but we need it now as much as ever.

She put two cups on the table, filled the first with scalding water, then poured the water back and forth between them, finally breaking brittle sachets of coffee and sugar crystals over each.

How old are you? she asked, pushing a mug toward me.

I told her. Nearly forty.

The *Thalassoma* years, she murmured—or that's how I heard it.

She took a blister pack from the carnival glass bowl, crushed a tablet of some kind between two tarnished spoons.

Life goes on a bit, she said, stirring the pulverized medication into her drink. Just so's you know. Life goes on quite a bit longer than most of us expect. Myself, I would've been perfectly happy with a three-act. Well, happy . . . In any case, three would've been perfectly sufficient. Never cared much for a five-acter. Same bones, only so much more waffling to lay them out. Same brontosaurus, however you rearrange it.

Had she been in the theater? I ventured.

Her laugh, gravelly, even when she said the word *Floss*. (I'm not sure she recalled my actual name.) No, Floss. Not the theater, not I. Only ever the cheap seats. Still, she said, dabbing up some stray granules with a licked fingertip. You do catch the whole show from the cheap seats; we've got that going for us. (Light found her eye, then.)

Outside, a wattlebird's throaty crackle. It was still black out there, but there was a little blue creeping into the darkness.

Astronomical twilight, Tilde said. If you could whistle, next time.

Whistle?

Or if you can't whistle . . .

I can sort of whistle.

I was going to say, if you can't whistle then sing something. So you don't startle the sweet loving fuck out of me.

. . .

Hard to fathom her laid up in the ICU, halfway to Melbourne, plugged in and inert. Wired up to machines. Not plausible. Easier to imagine her walking the halls like a task-hungry ghost, trailing her IV and oxygen tank and looking for something to fix. Or irritably disentangling herself from the net of breathing and feeding tubes and breaking loose, Tilde doing Tilde, go to whoa.

But even if, when she does shake this thing, chances are she'll only make it as far as aged care.

What will happen to it all, if she never makes it back—the carriage, her trees, whatever's going on below? Who does it fall to?

No family that we know of, and few you could really call close. Thorpe. Ourselves. The sculptor, Janine, whom she swaps tools and seeds and grafting tips with, and the man who rides the train up from Melbourne a couple of times a year. Her young friend, Tilde calls him when pressed. Theo, when pressed a bit further. But you can never get much out of her beyond that.

He doesn't look so much younger than herself, not to our eyes. Fifteen years or so. Though it's clear they've led very different lives; you could just look at his hands. Elegant, you might call him, his hands and everything else. We'd seen them sitting together at the better of the town's two cafés. An outdoor table, out of range of all the ears. Their heads bent toward each other like conspiring parakeets. She looked different at these times, with him. Younger herself, her face and hands alive, alight in a new way. Well, and her hot chocolate likely "improved," spiked with something. She hardly ever went there otherwise, unless to nick sugar.

He might have been an actor. He'd make sense as an actor. His startling eyes and beautiful suits. A heavy, expensive-looking watch he had a habit of taking off and laying face down on the table, in the way I once saw a magician do shortly before beating it to pieces with a hammer. Who taught him to do this, I wondered. Needless to say, no hammer in this instance. I know what he meant by it was: there is nothing more important, no call to make, no train to miss. But the gesture still made me think perhaps she knew him from the theater.

That, and she's never troubled to introduce him. To me or anyone, not even Maree. As if keeping him just for herself.

• • •

The last time I found her at home, Tilde was outside, stoking kindling beneath the ancient clawfoot firebath she used in all seasons.

The dog left my heel and bolted straight over to the bright, dog-beautiful patch of soft new green, Tilde watching after her, cagily, I thought.

She's really more of a musterer than a digger, I reassured. Mama was a shepherd.

Who was Papa? Tilde asked, unconvinced.

We don't know about Papa, I admitted.

Well, she said, softening a little. Sometimes that's for the best.

Steam was beginning to rise from the iron-pawed

tub. She crouched to redistribute the coals, then stood upright and dusted soot from her hands, looking back to where the dog was stretched out regal as Anubis on the verdant rug of turf.

So she told you about it, I suppose. (She meant Maree.)

How do you mean? I asked, though I knew she meant the bunker.

Everybody in town knew about the bunker. Everybody knew there was more to it. Though it was true she believed in nigh times and spoke half in Yeats, Tilde was still sharp enough to know that seventy-year-old steel under a few feet of earth wasn't going to withstand much of anything—wasn't going to dampen an inferno, or slow the creep of radiation by so much as a becquerel.

She believed otherwise, though. Believed the horse float was as good as consecrated. It had carried a child-saint down the west coast, half a century ago, and hadn't been tainted with anything or anyone else since.

(Maree had not, in fact, told me this last part.)

Three rounds of fires had swept through the region in the years since she'd buried it, and wind-borne embers from surrounding blazes had singed not a stick, not a leaf, sparing the grove and her home within it.

What does that tell you?

I couldn't say. Flame retardant, those trees?

Blessed, she hissed. Holy.

I wanted to know where the saint was now, but Tilde waved a hand; what did that matter?

I don't keep up with the itineraries of saints, she said, and I could see she was already sorry that she'd told me.

Perhaps to keep me from prying any further, or to hustle me along, she asked where my woman was, when she would be coming back.

Across the ditch, I told her, Palmerston.

I understood I was being dismissed, and said I'd better get back to catch Maree's call.

I called out to the dog. She pricked her ears at her name, then got up slowly, obedient but far from keen, holding out for particulars.

She lifted each paw deliberately, as if she had started to put down roots, then stood waiting for clearer direction.

Kiko, I said again. Here now. Hometime.

• • •

Someone from the town will come for it sooner or later. Saint or no. Churn the ground up, see what Tilde's idea of treasure had been.

I've thought myself of taking a spade and slicing up the clods until I feel the knock travel up through my forearms, until the muffled knell of hollow metal.

And I've thought better of it. Again and again.

There's supposedly a hatch to it somewhere, sealed over now with turf and layers of decaying leaflitter. I find this both comforting and terrible.

Alone in Tilde's home I lay my palms flat upon the plastic gingham tablecloth. Feel them stick. Wanting something to call Holy, call Hallowed, but without all the rest of the bullshit, if you please.

Outside, against the green, the russet streak of the dog, after something. She howls once, a deep animal keening that spills into the furrows of my own and makes us complicit.

I learn Tilde's full name from her prescription labels. Take out my phone and look up:

eletriptan for heartbreak
propranolol for heartbreak

I swallow a couple of each, tipping a sugar sachet into my mouth after to draw off the bitterness.

In a dream I had recently I could see Tilde just as she was, not draped weightless upon an ICU bed but here still, living below, just as hardy and hoary as ever, drawing sustenance from the underworld. Gnawing tubers, tapping roots for their sugared water, light channeled down through the filaments of her grove, the python-patterned trunks of her miraculous trees.

That's not quite true, about it coming in a dream. It's an image summoned up in broad daylight—lucid, sober—and seeming no more implausible than anything else.

I could come right out and ask her, ask Tilde:
Are we in the Before or the After?

Acknowledgments

Thank you, Claudia Ballard, for so thoroughly embracing this book exactly as it arrived, and through all its shape-shifting thereafter.

Thanks to Ashley Nelson Levy and Adam Levy, and all at Transit Books for the warmth, generosity, and vision brought to the US edition. Thank you, Jared Bartman, for the perfect cover.

Thanks to Chris Feik, Jo Rosenberg, and all at Black Inc. in Australia.

I'm deeply grateful for the generous early reads and many other kindnesses that have carried me through writing and all else, especially during the last couple of coastal years—Madeleine Thien & Julia Foulkes & Nara Milanich, Jo Canham, Rodney Hall, Kate Rendell, Lisa Lang & Romy Ash & Laura Jean McKay & Anna Krien, Wayne Macauley, Vanessa & Neil Boyack, Angela Meyer, Jonathan Batten, Leith Maguire, Dean Mundey,

Sharyn Jencke & Ian Hill, Steven Amsterdam & Corry de Neef, Mireille Juchau, Sarah Holland-Batt, Michelle de Kretser.

Steven Bird, for invaluable insights and delible green, David Burrows (XVI & XVII), Paul Spencer (ibid.).

Thank you, Madeleine Thien (once again).

Thank you, Patrick Pittman, North Star, for all the years of your friendship, love, and wisdom.

"Tamanu" was first published as "Little World" in *Zoetrope: All-Story* (Fall 2022), and appeared subsequently in *New Australian Fiction* and *The Monthly*. An earlier version of "Bunker" first appeared in *Australian Book Review*. My thanks to the editors of these publications for their time, care, and influence.

JOSEPHINE ROWE was born in 1984 in Rockhampton, Australia, and grew up in Melbourne. She is the author of three story collections and two novels, including *A Loving, Faithful Animal*, longlisted for the 2017 Miles Franklin Literary Award and selected as a *New York Times* Editors' Choice. She has twice been named a *Sydney Morning Herald* Best Young Australian Novelist, and her collection *Here Until August* was shortlisted for the 2020 Stella Prize. Rowe has held fellowships from the International Writing Program at the University of Iowa, the Wallace Stegner Fellowship at Stanford University, and the Dorothy and Lewis B. Cullman Center at the New York Public Library, among others. She currently lives in coastal Victoria.

Transit Books is a nonprofit publisher of international and American literature, based in the San Francisco Bay Area. Founded in 2015, Transit Books is committed to the discovery and promotion of enduring works that carry readers across borders and communities. Visit us online to learn more about our forthcoming titles, events, and opportunities to support our mission.

TRANSITBOOKS.ORG